Goldilocks
and the
Three Bears

tiger tales

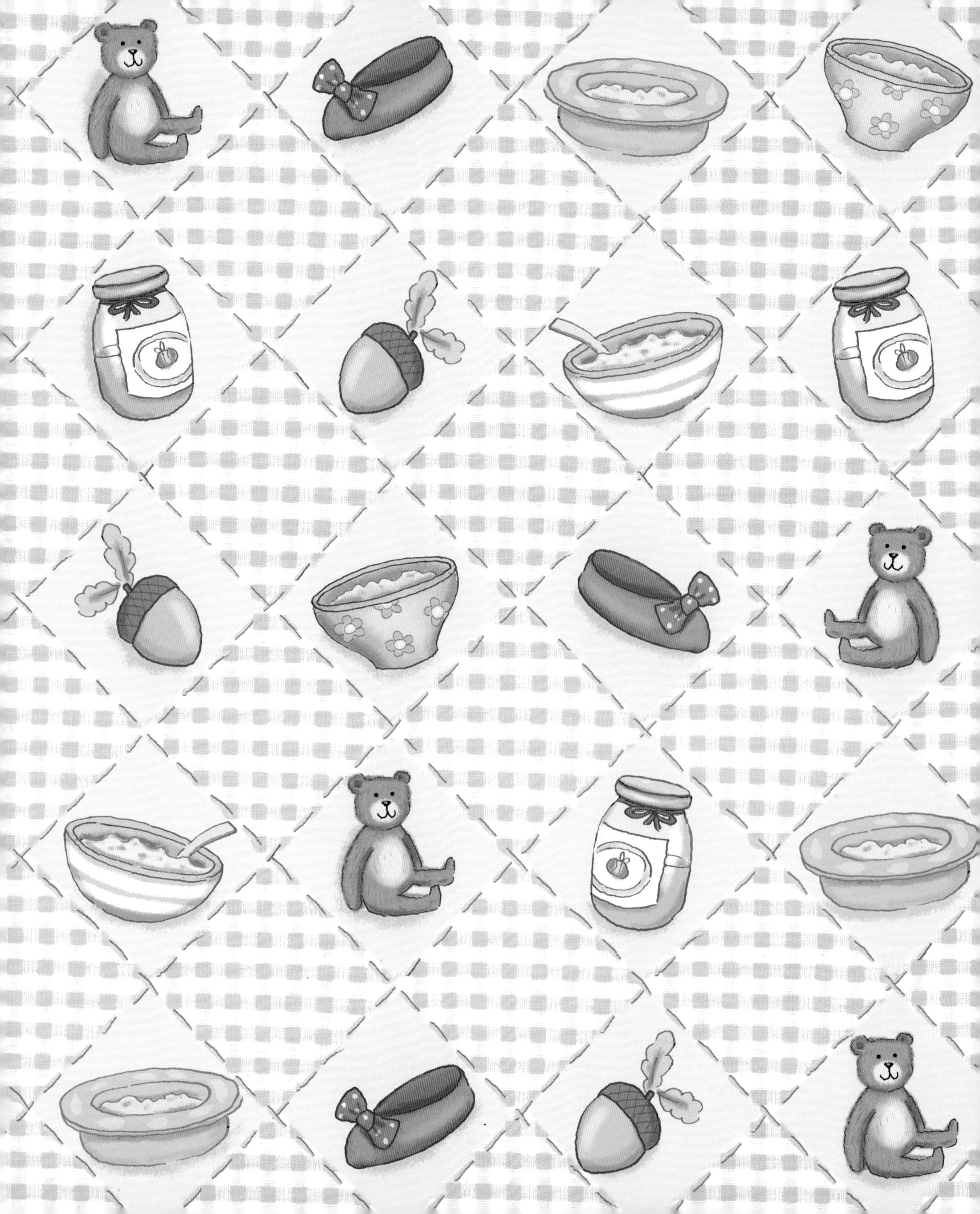

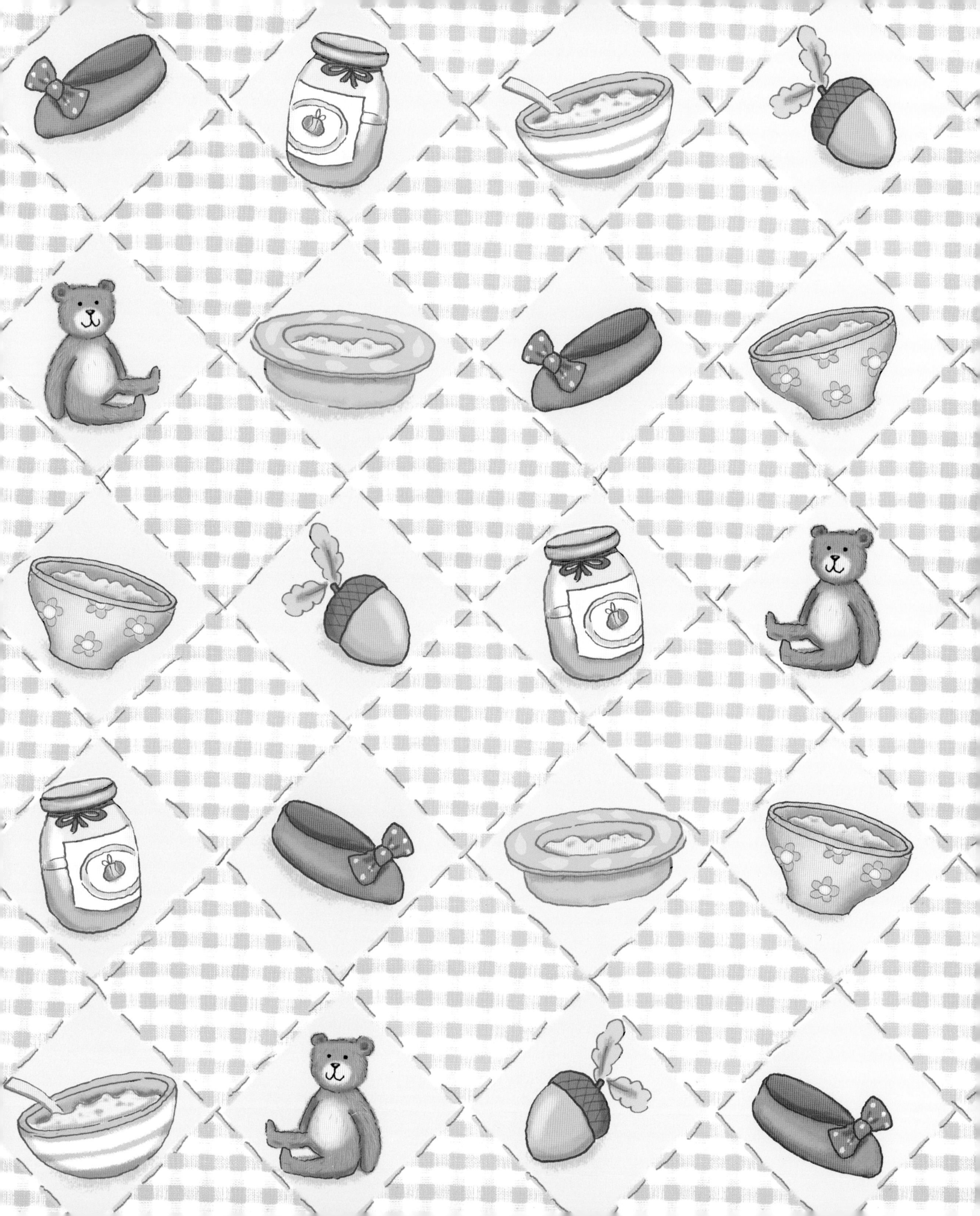

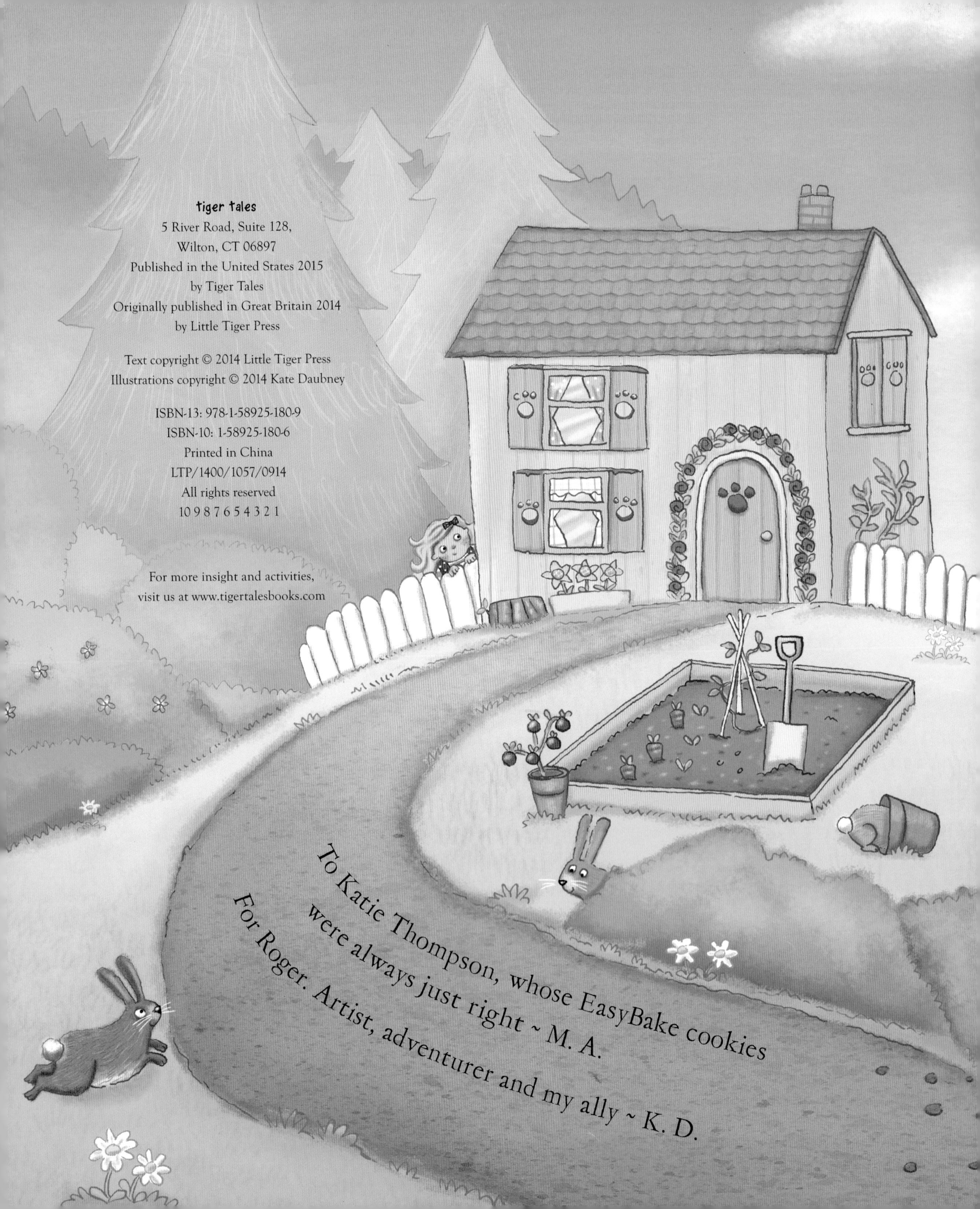

tiger tales
5 River Road, Suite 128,
Wilton, CT 06897
Published in the United States 2015
by Tiger Tales
Originally published in Great Britain 2014
by Little Tiger Press

ISBN-13: 978-1-58925-180-9
ISBN-10: 1-58925-180-6
Printed in China
LTP/1400/1057/0914

10 9 8 7 6 5 4 3 2 1

For more insight and activities,
visit us at www.tigertalesbooks.com

To Katie Thompson, whose EasyBake cookies
were always just right ~ M. A.
For Roger. Artist, adventurer and my ally ~ K. D.

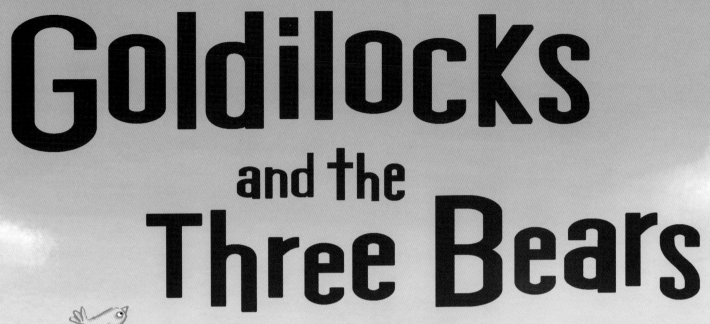

Goldilocks
and the
Three Bears

adapted by Mara Alperin

Illustrated by Kate Daubney

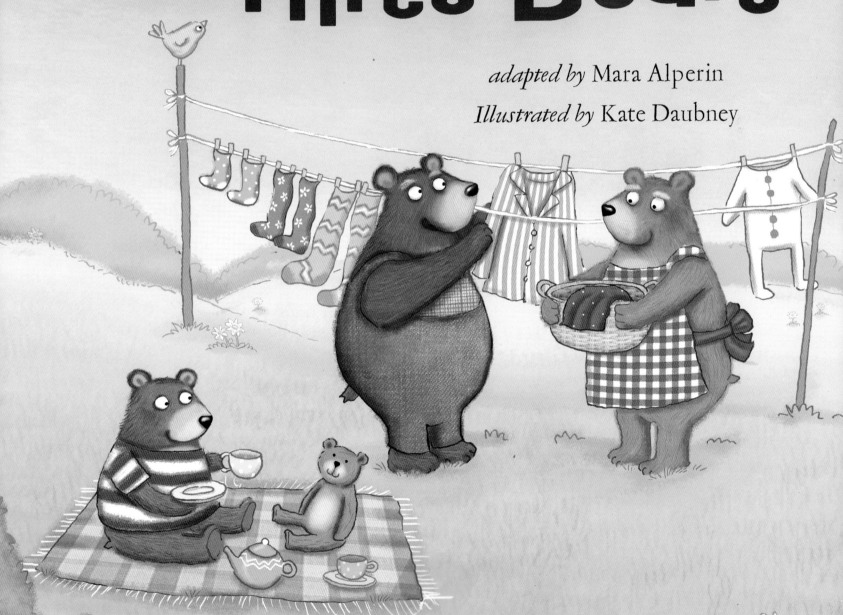

tiger tales

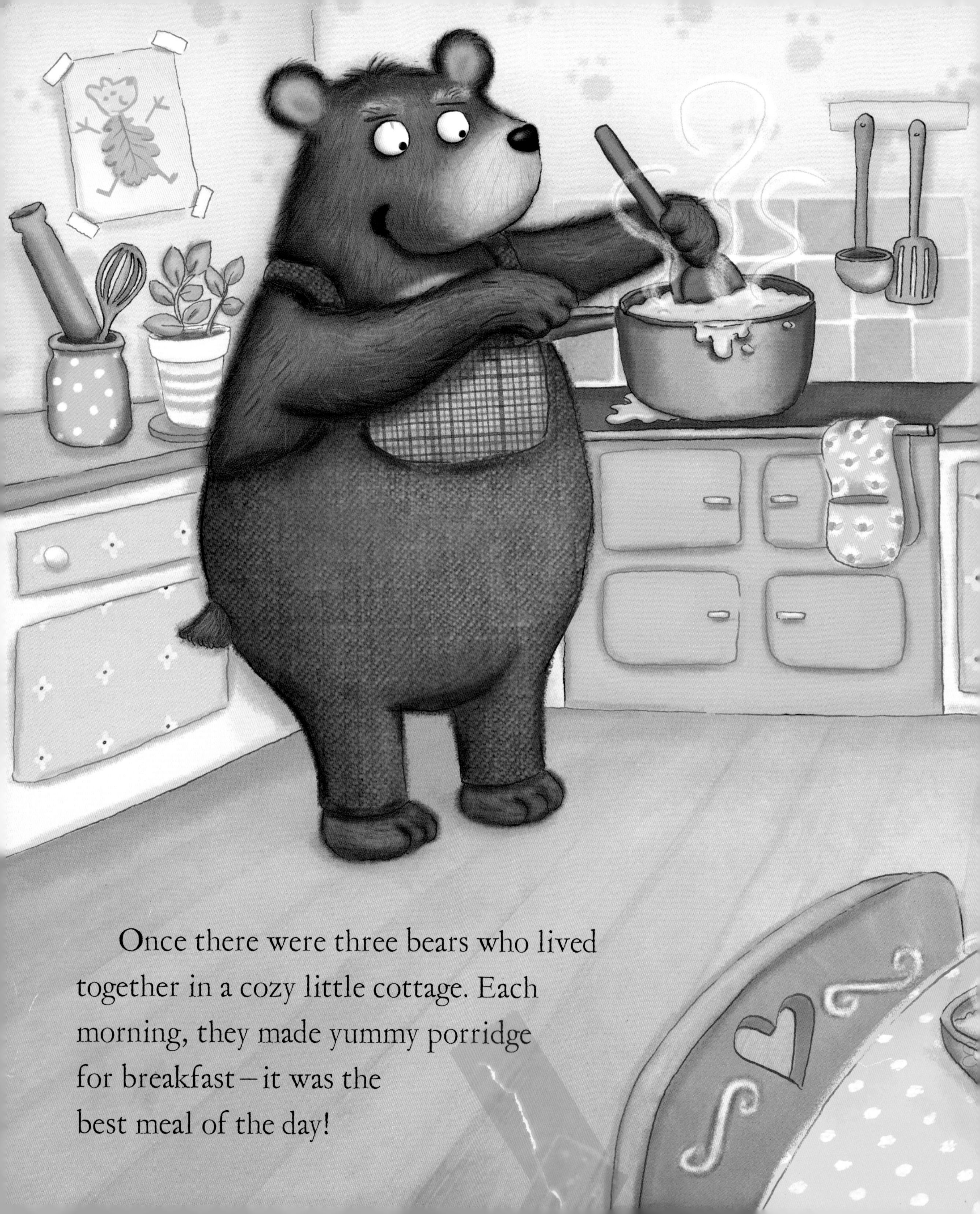

Once there were three bears who lived together in a cozy little cottage. Each morning, they made yummy porridge for breakfast—it was the best meal of the day!

But one morning, Baby Bear said, "Ouch! This porridge is hot-hot-hot!"

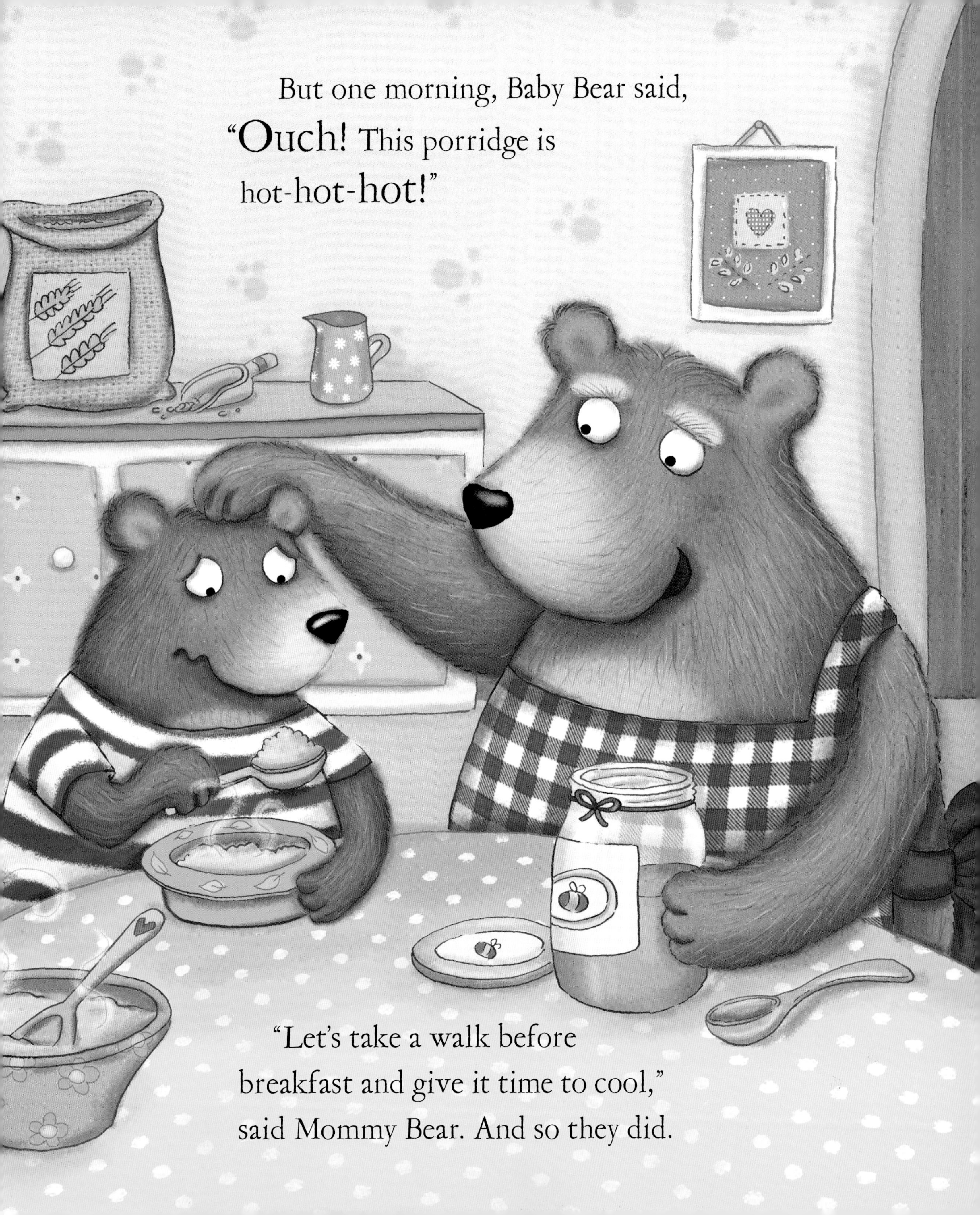

"Let's take a walk before breakfast and give it time to cool," said Mommy Bear. And so they did.

No sooner had the bears left than someone peeked in through the window – someone with bright, golden hair. Her name was Goldilocks . . . and she was a very curious little girl!

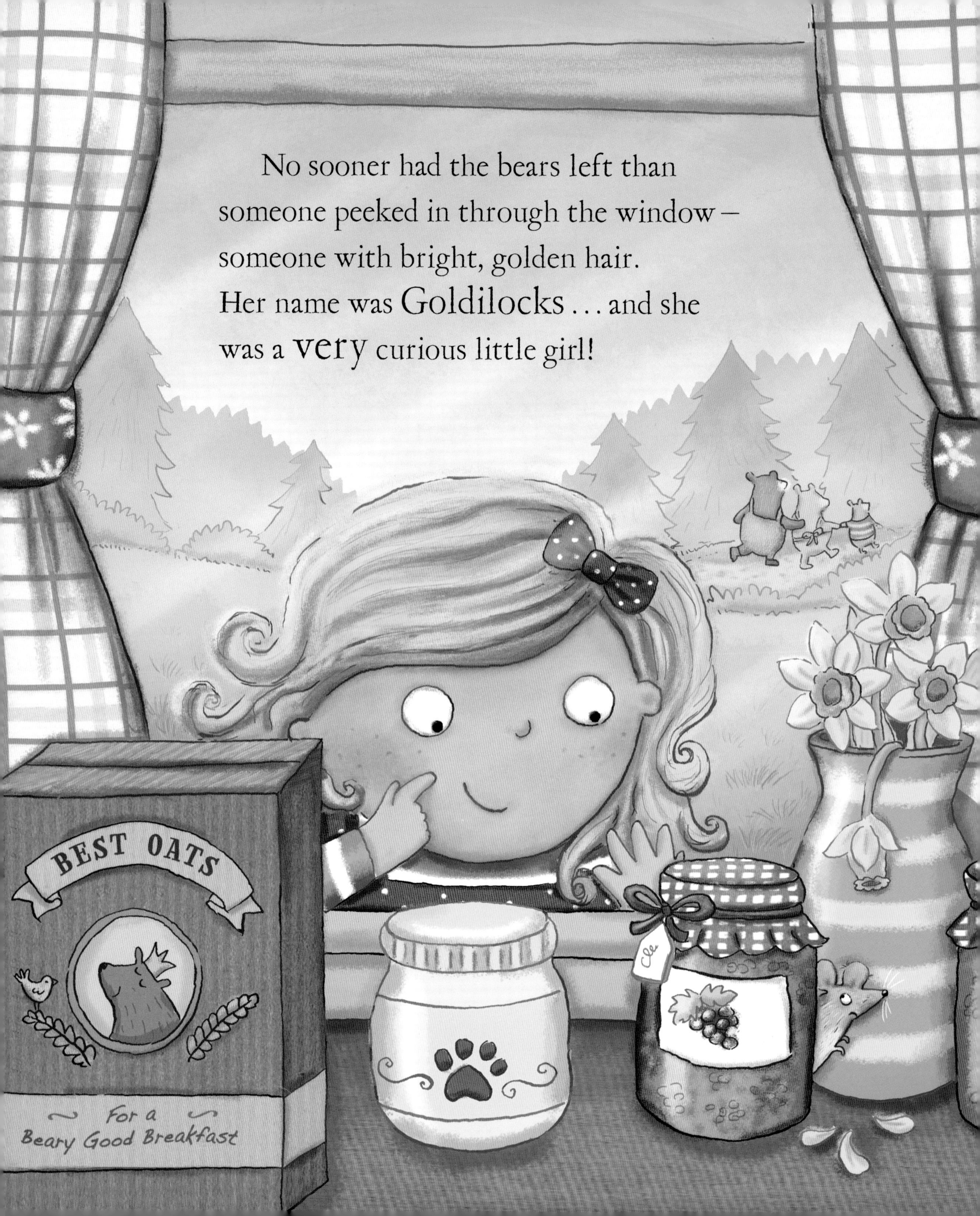
BEST OATS
For a
Beary Good Breakfast

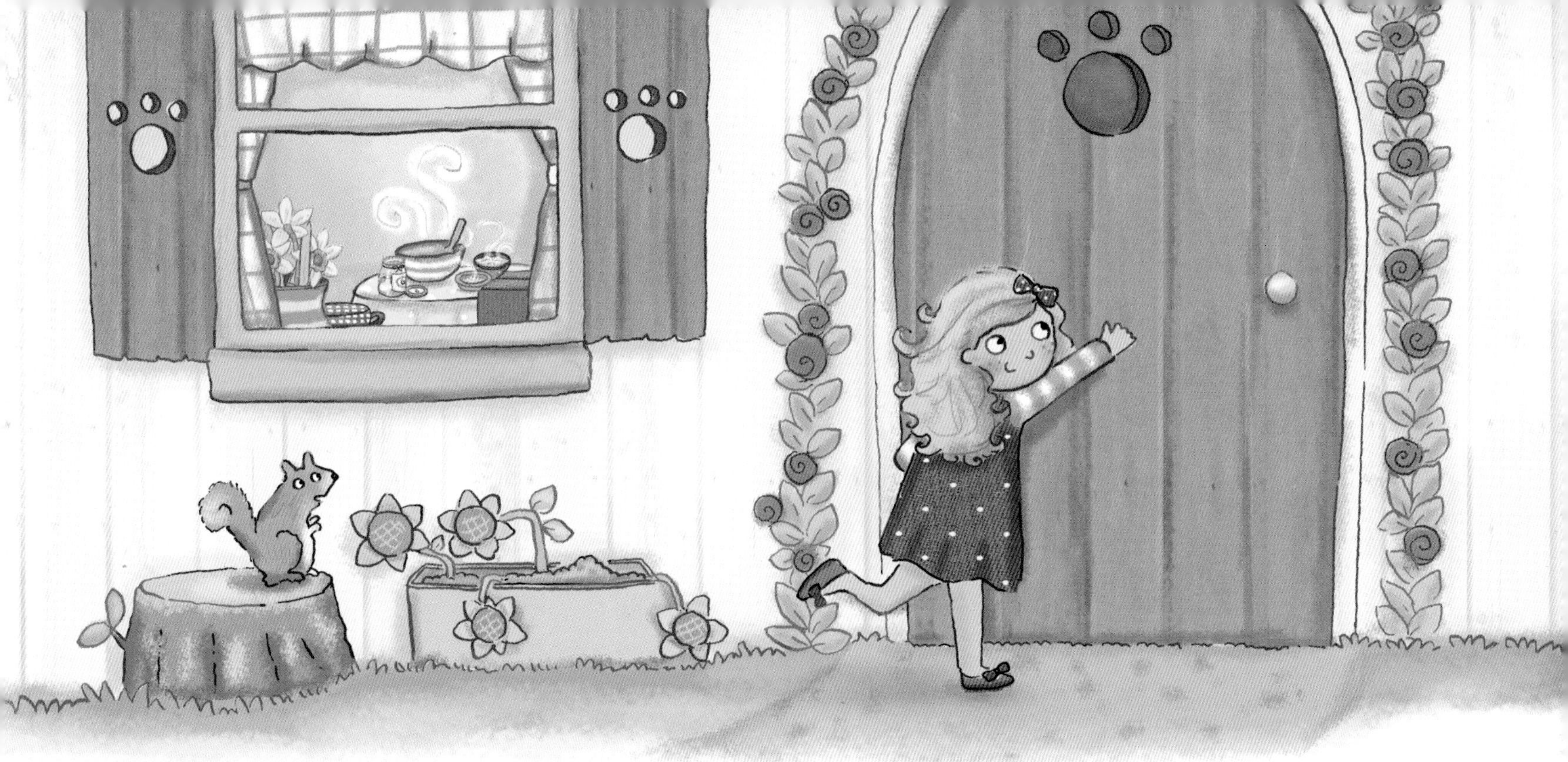

Goldilocks tap-tap-**tapped** on the door.

"Hello?" she called.

"Hellooo?"

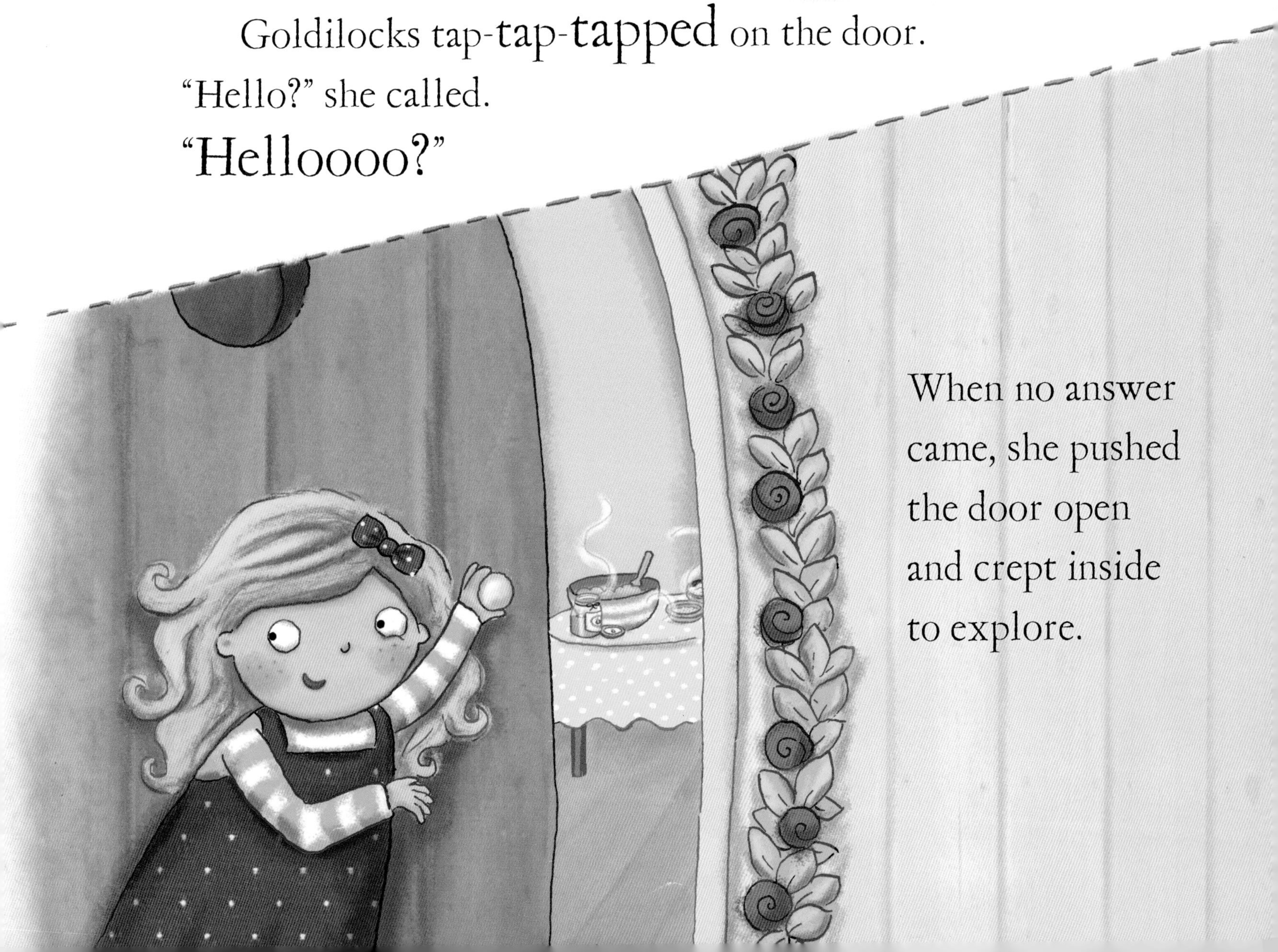

When no answer came, she pushed the door open and crept inside to explore.

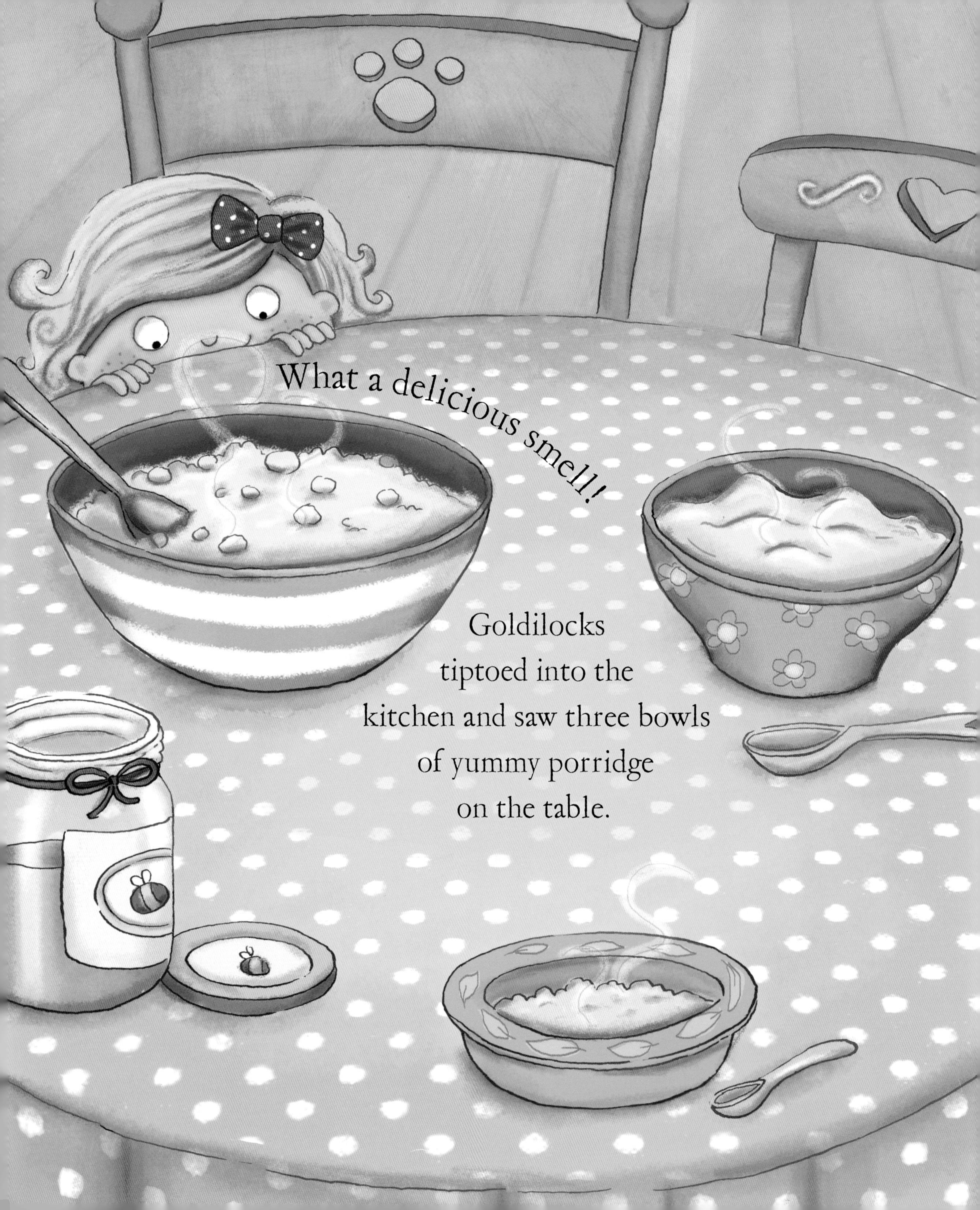

What a delicious smell!

Goldilocks tiptoed into the kitchen and saw three bowls of yummy porridge on the table.

She slurped Daddy Bear's porridge, but it was too lumpy.

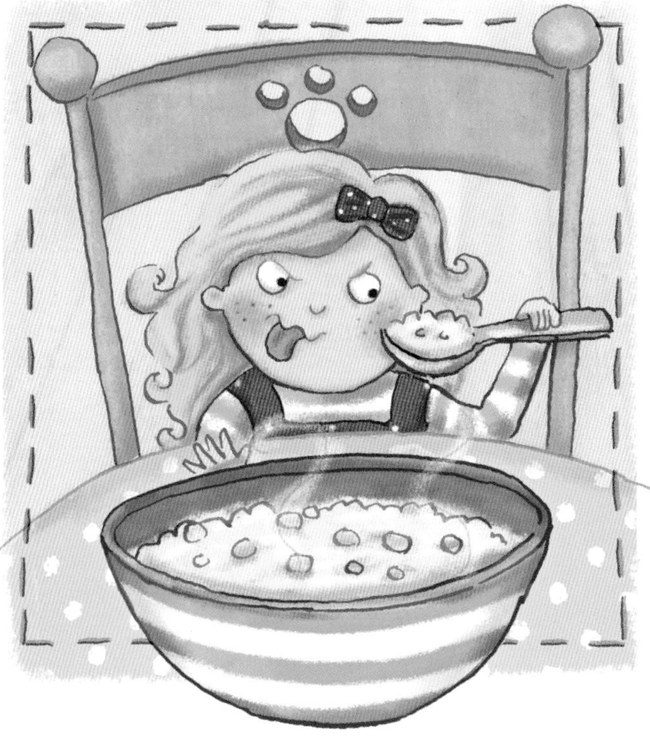

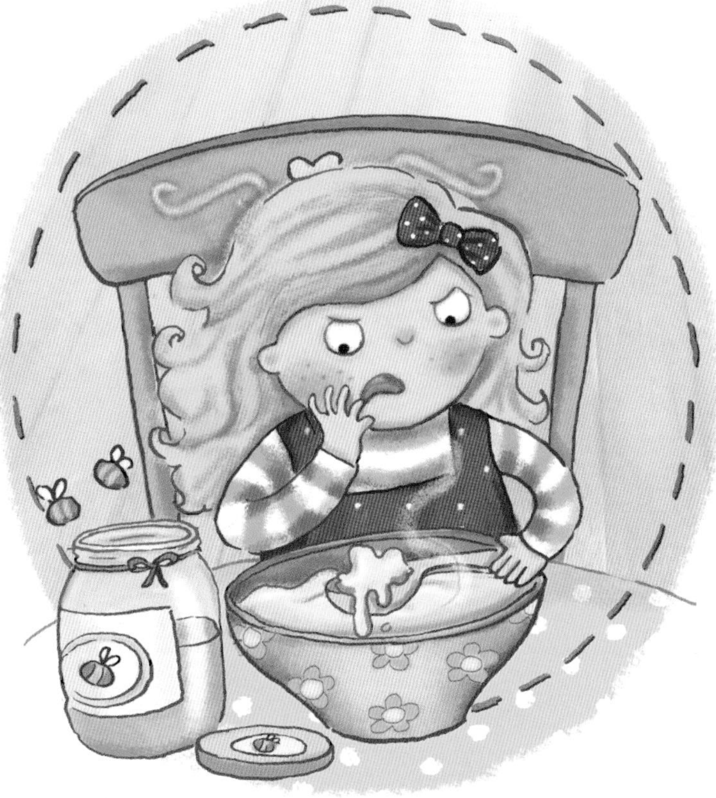

She sipped Mommy Bear's porridge, but it was too sweet.

Then she tasted Baby Bear's porridge. It was just right...

so she ate it all up!

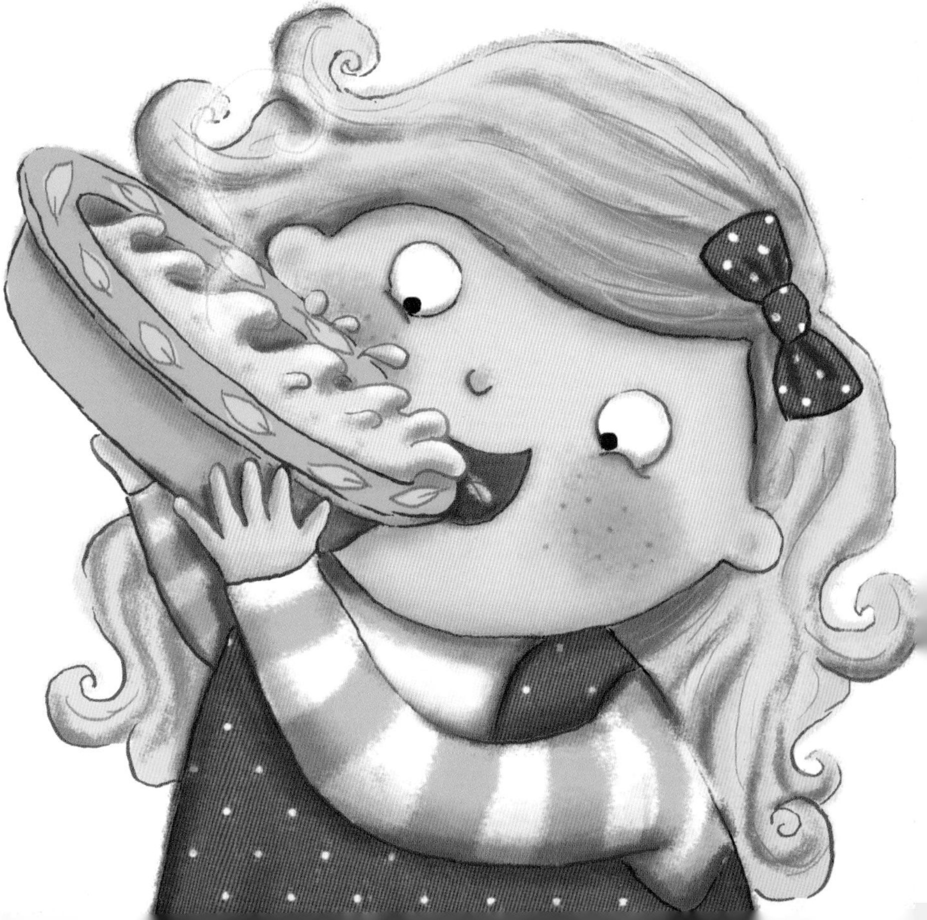

Goldilocks was very full, so she looked around for somewhere to sit. There in the living room were three **magnificent** chairs.

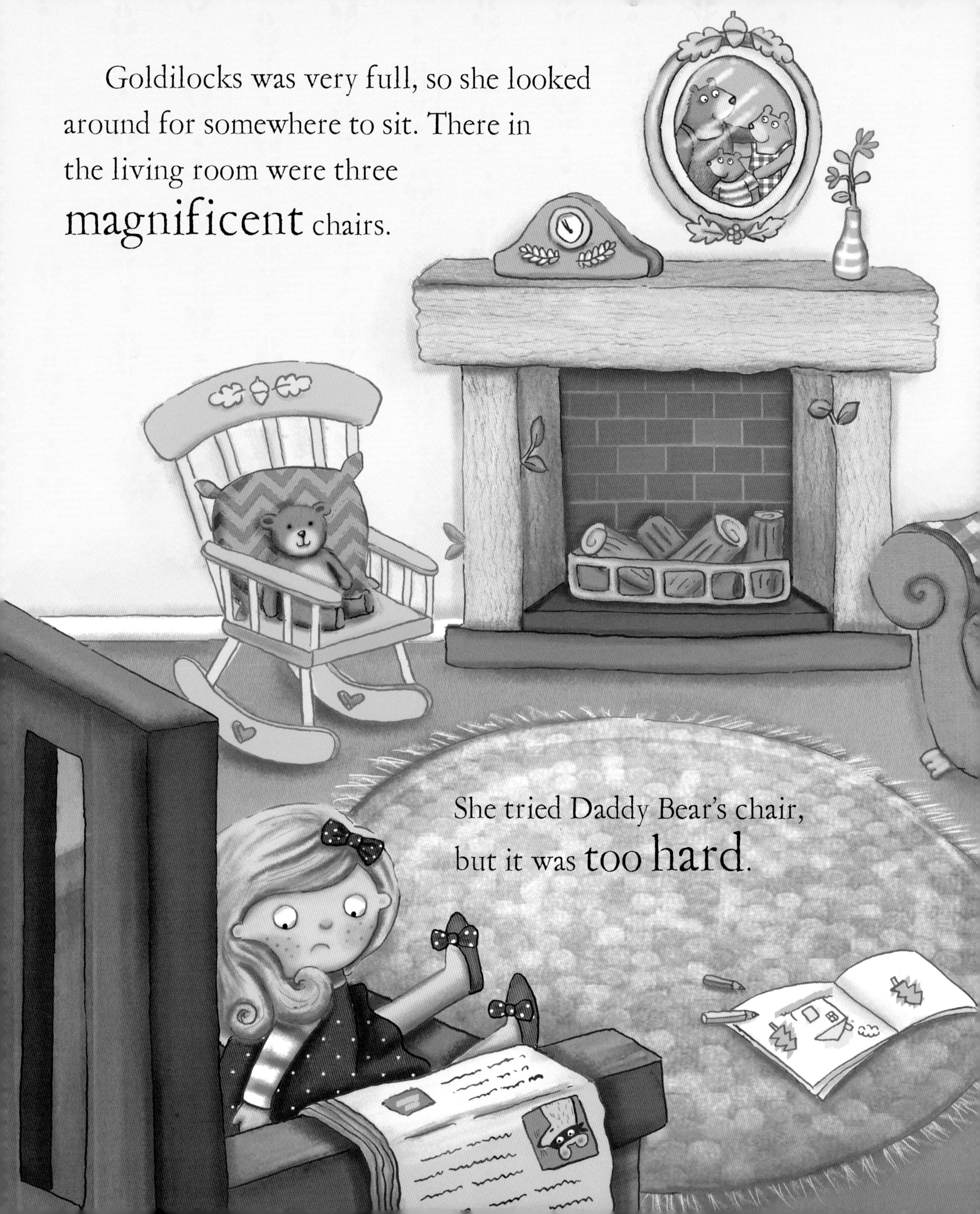

She tried Daddy Bear's chair, but it was **too hard**.

She squished into
Mommy Bear's chair,
but it was **too soft**.

Then she rocked in Baby Bear's
chair. It was just **right** . . . .

"Wheee!" cried Goldilocks. She rocked
and rocked, **faster** and **faster**, until . . .

CRASH!

went the chair, and broke into a hundred pieces.

"Oops!" giggled Goldilocks.

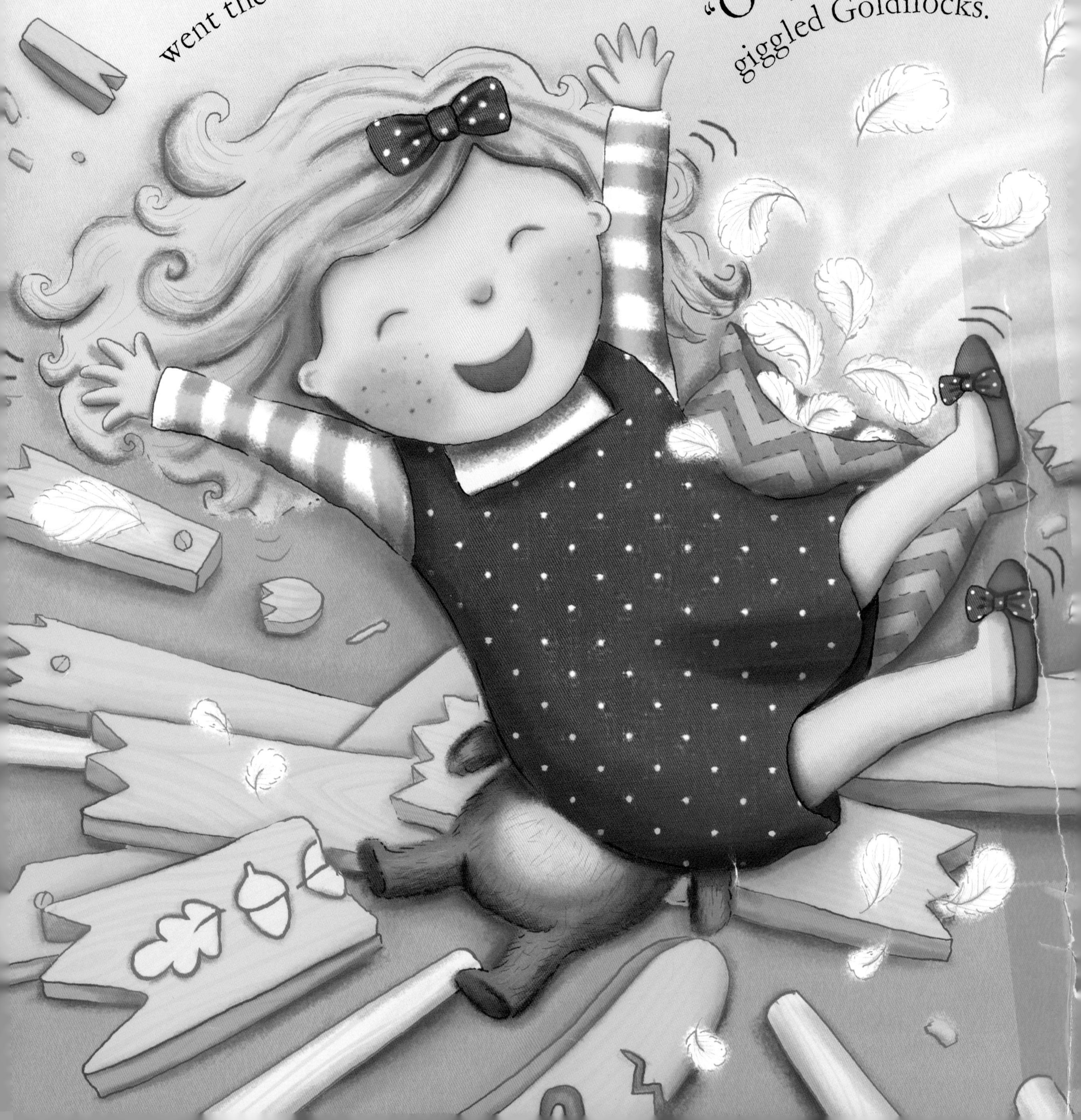

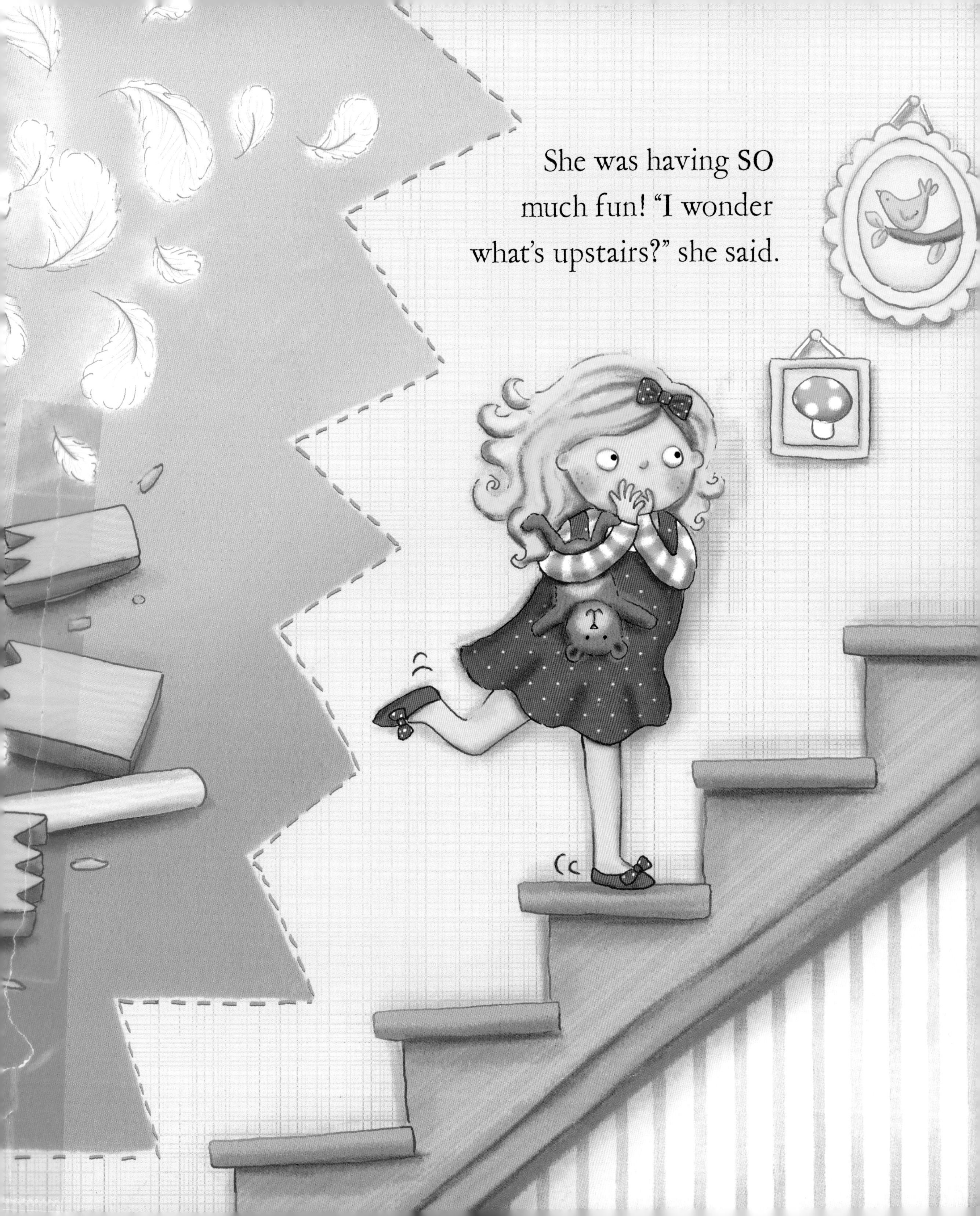

She was having SO
much fun! "I wonder
what's upstairs?" she said.

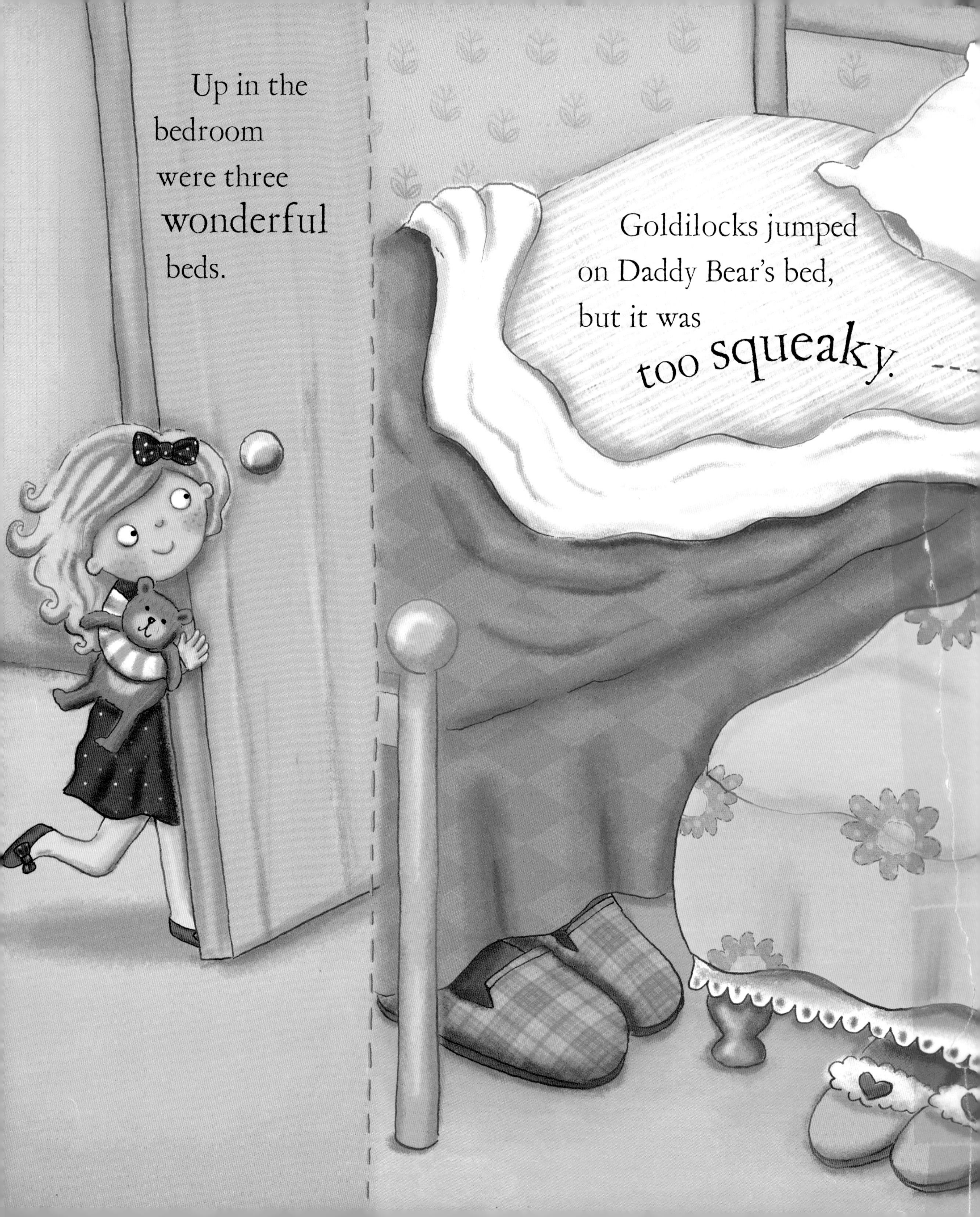

Up in the bedroom were three **wonderful** beds.

Goldilocks jumped on Daddy Bear's bed, but it was too squeaky.

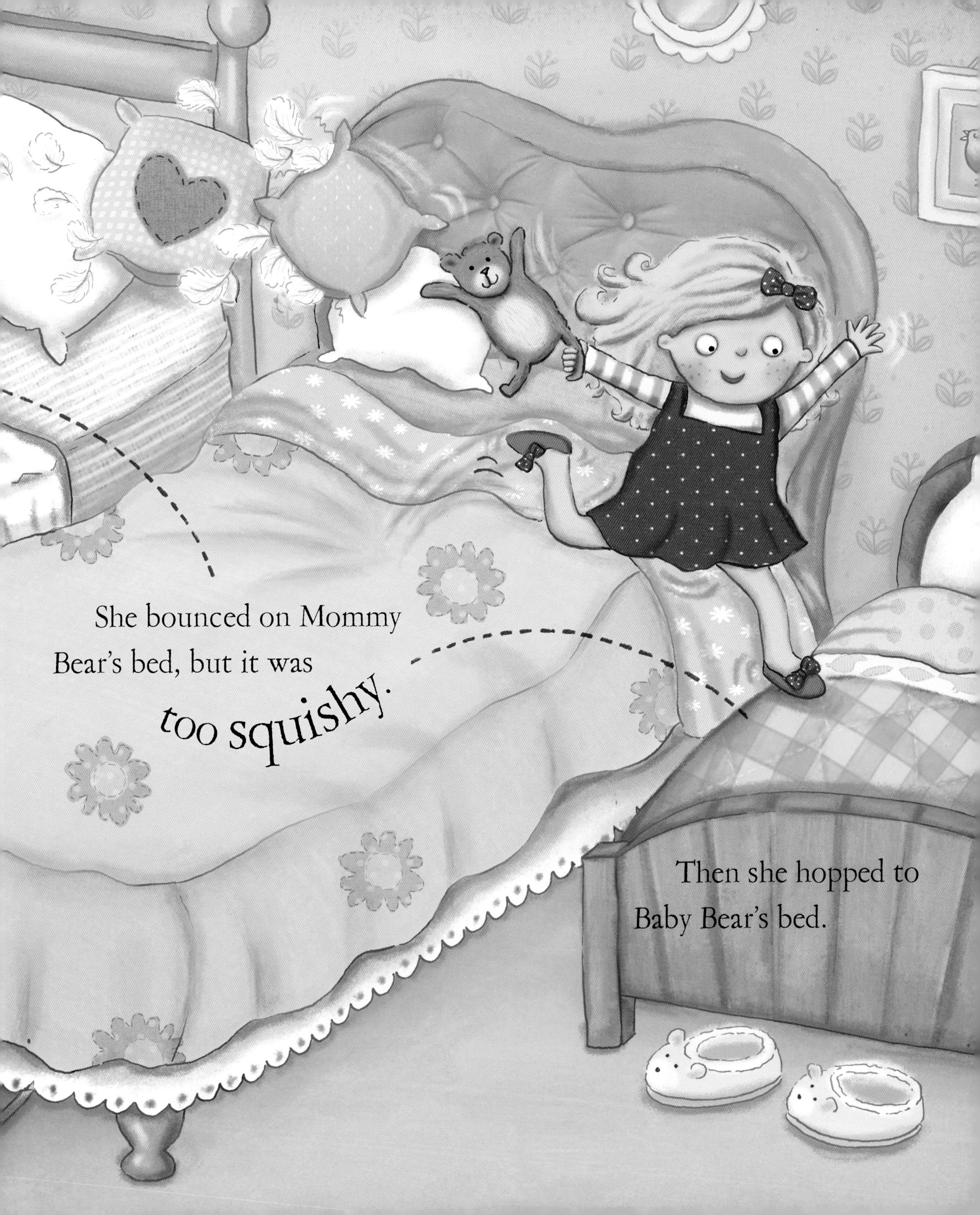

She bounced on Mommy Bear's bed, but it was too squishy.

Then she hopped to Baby Bear's bed.

It was just **right** . . .

"ZZZZZzzzzzzzzzzz!"

snored Goldilocks.

She had fallen fast asleep!

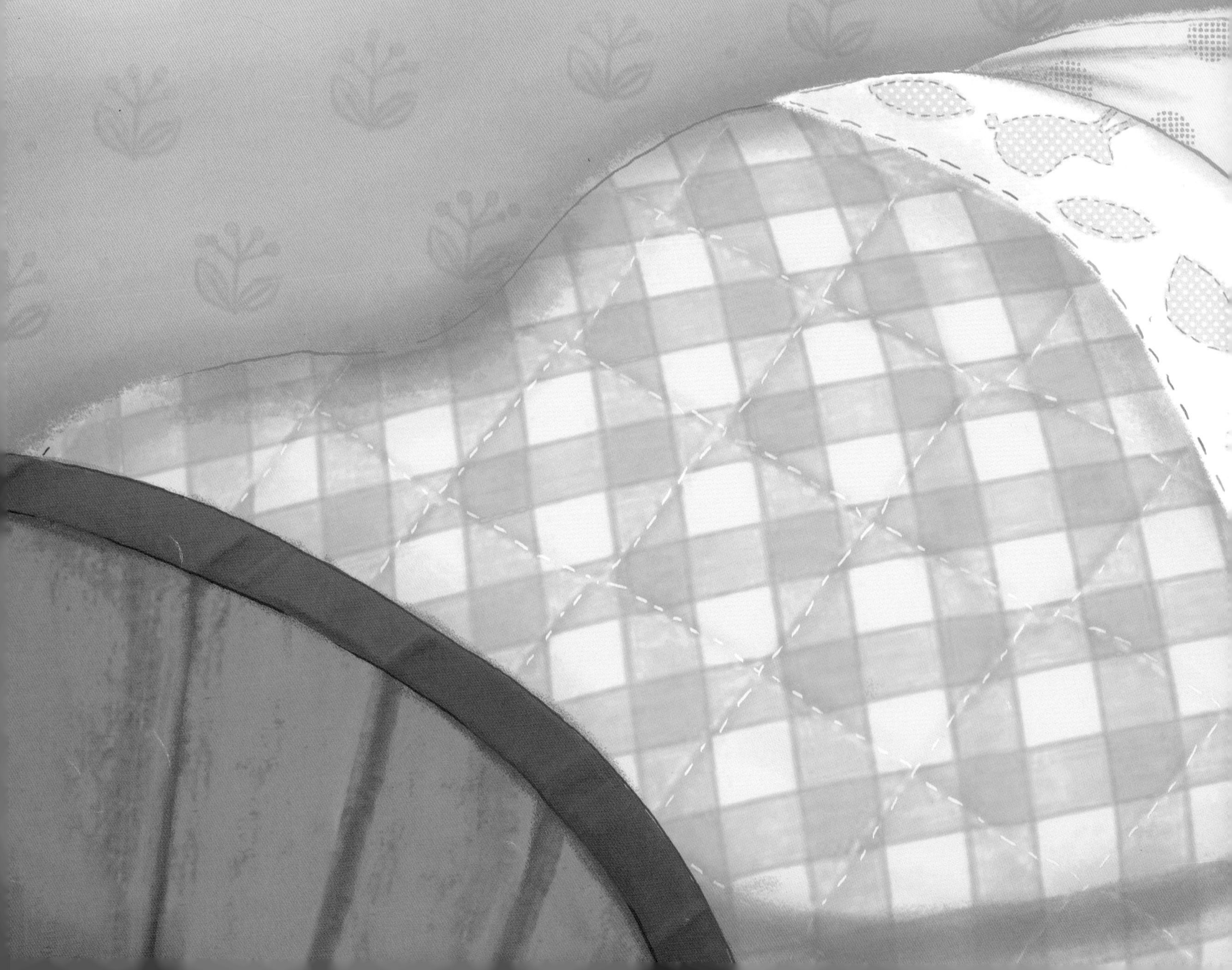

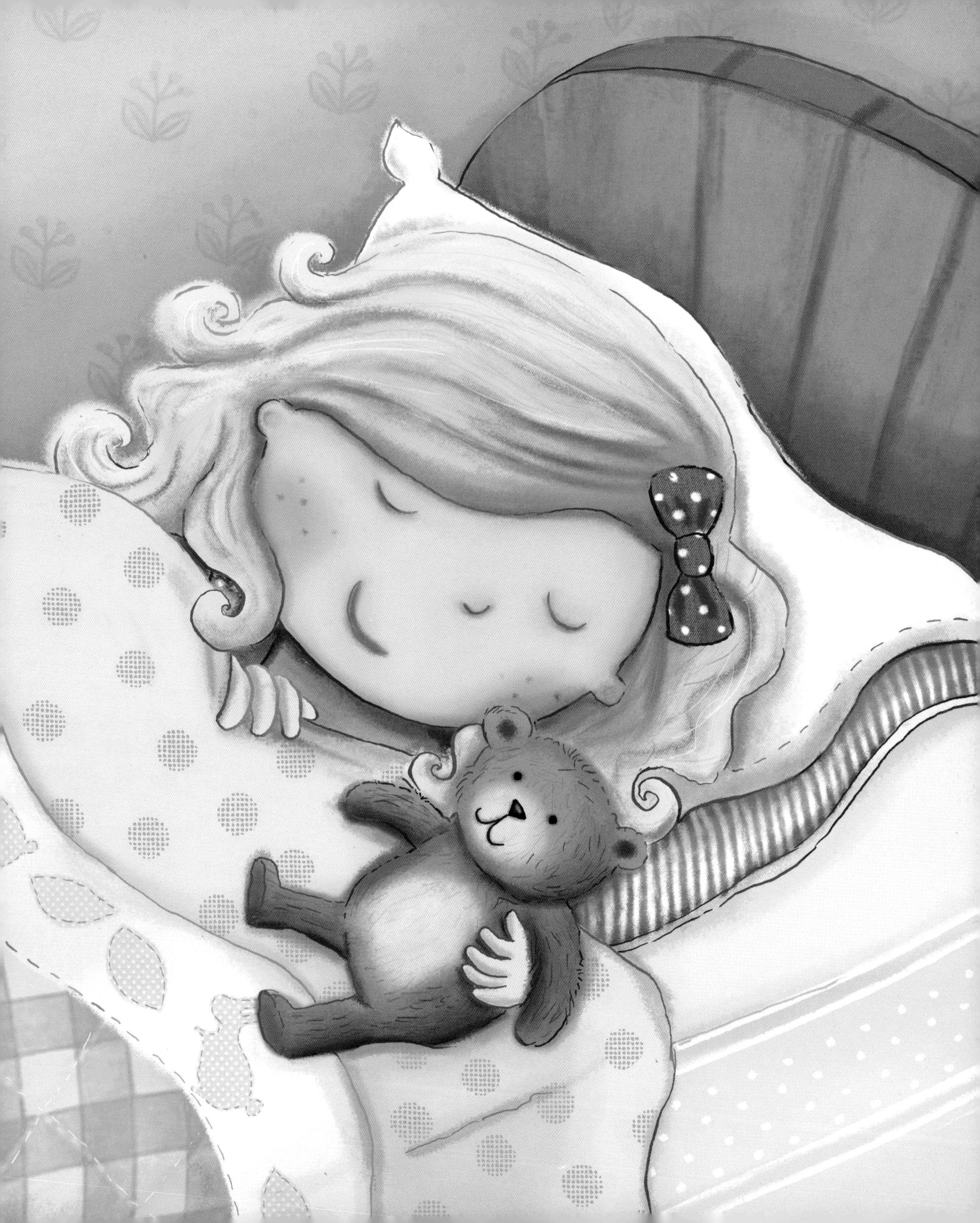

But as Goldilocks slept, the three bears came home. They were very, very hungry. And when they opened the door . . . .

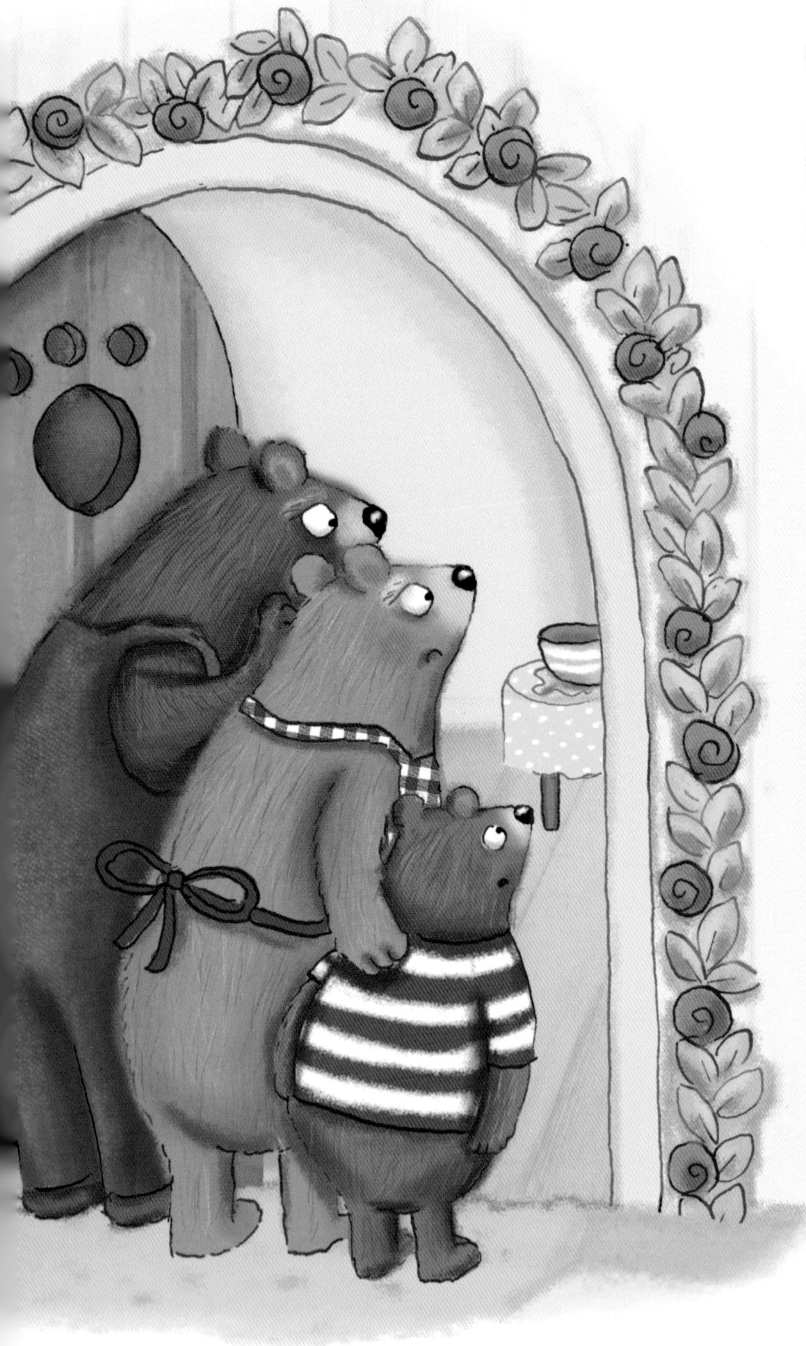

"Someone's been eating my porridge," growled Daddy Bear.

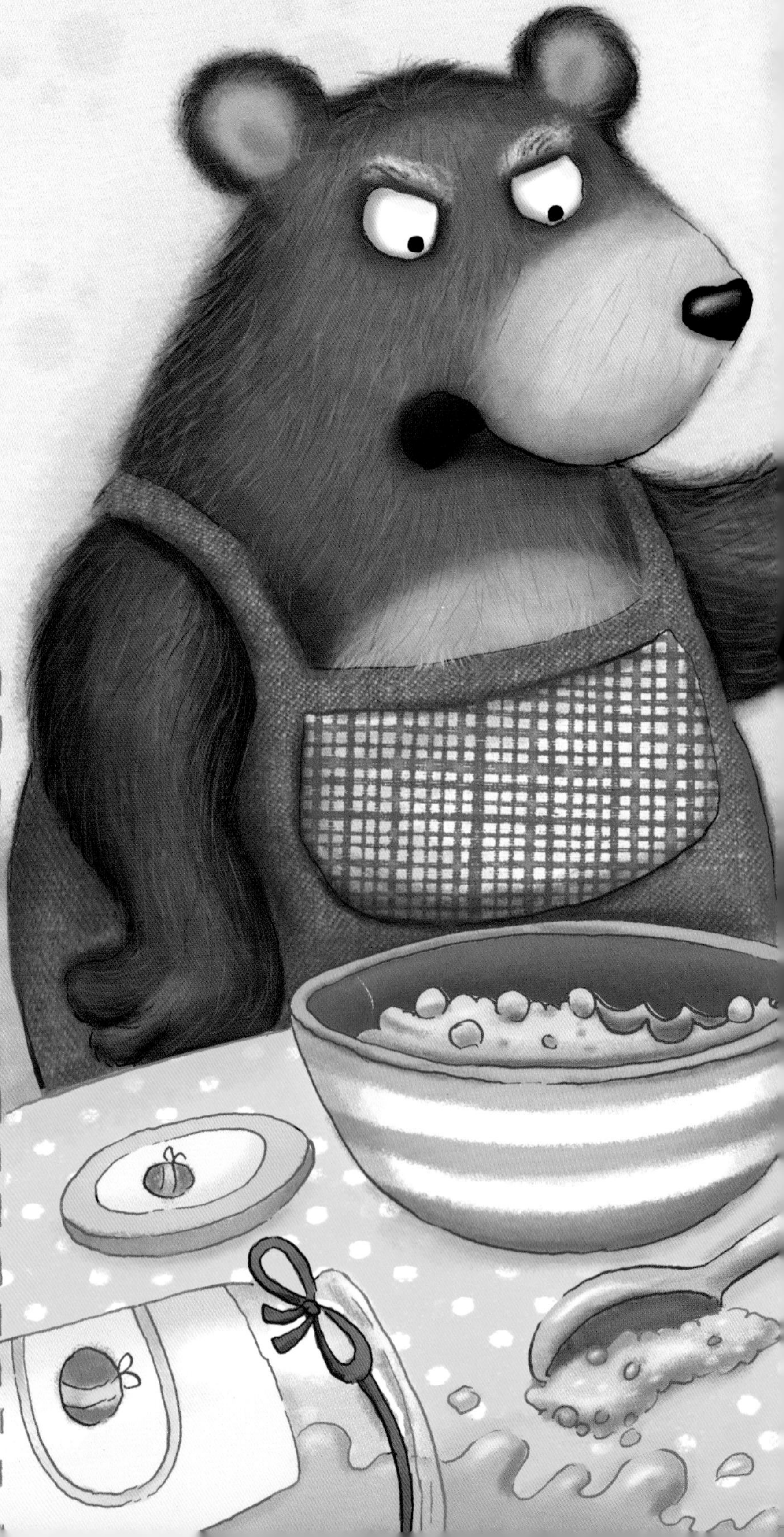

"Someone's been eating my porridge," gasped Mommy Bear.

"Someone's been eating my porridge," cried Baby Bear. "And now it's all gone!"

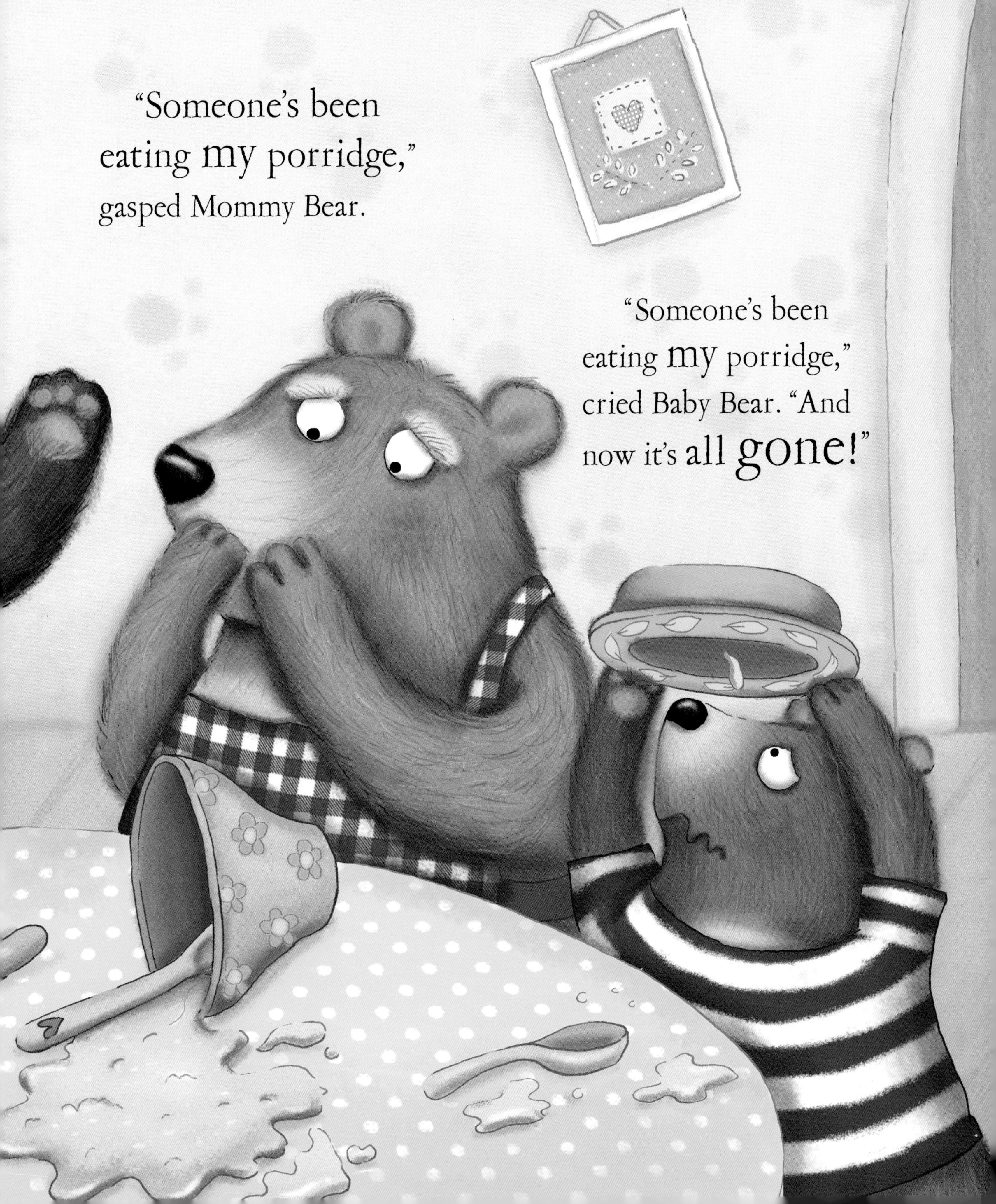

And before Mommy Bear could make some more porridge, they heard a loud ROAR from the living room.

"Someone's been sitting in my chair," growled Daddy Bear.

"Someone's been sitting in my chair," gasped Mommy Bear, rushing over.

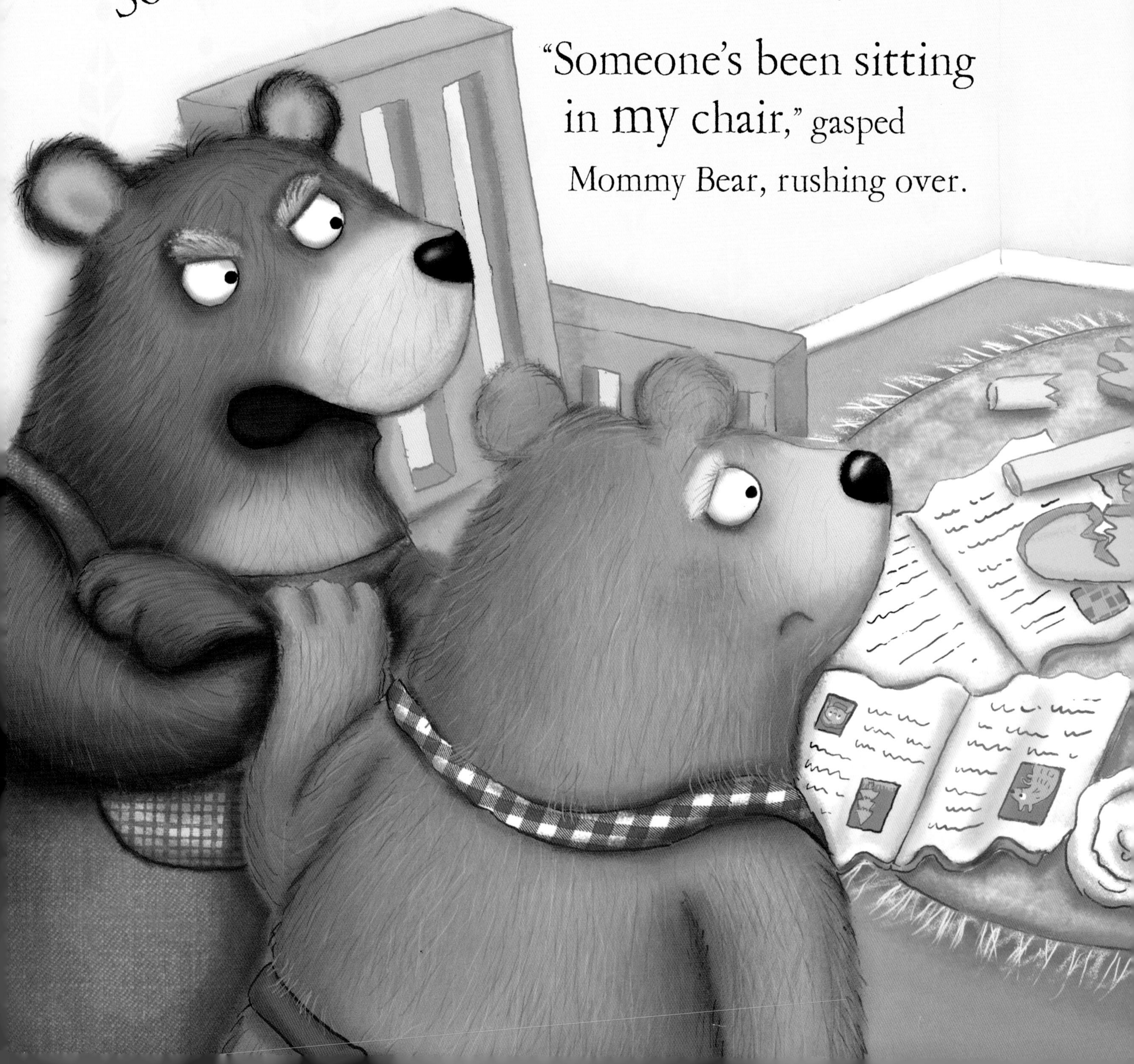

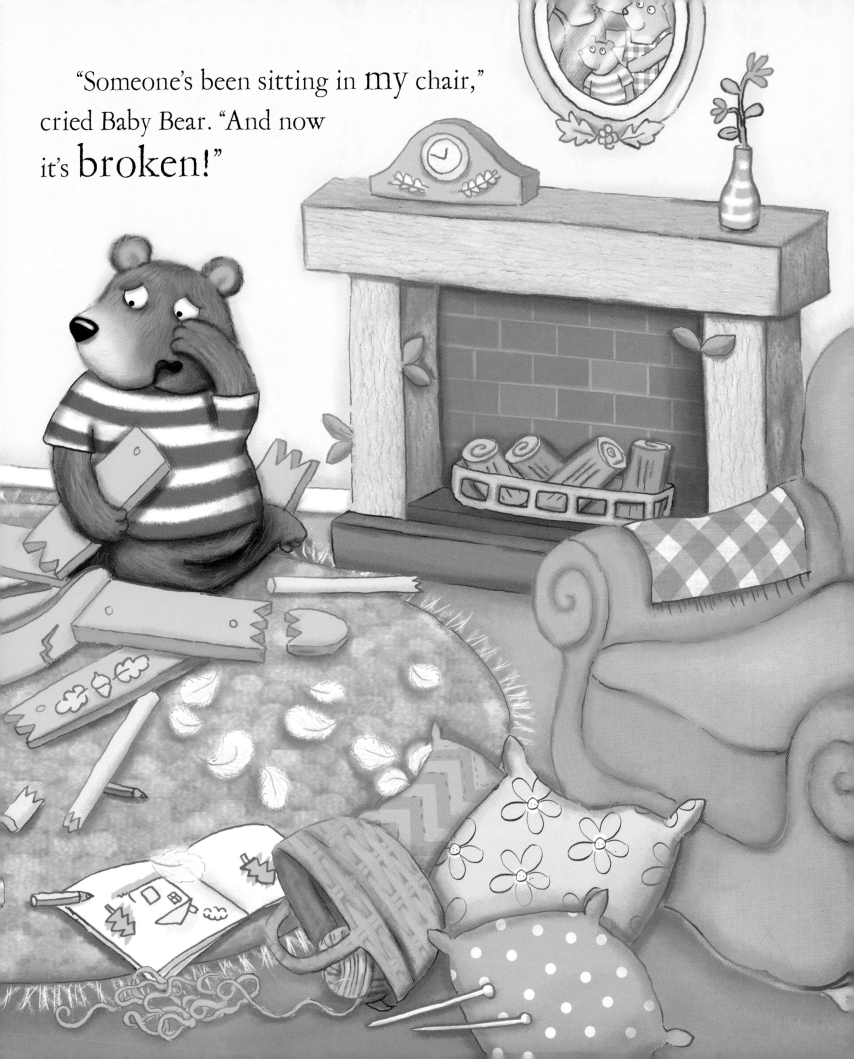

"Someone's been sitting in my chair," cried Baby Bear. "And now it's broken!"

But before Daddy Bear could fix the chair, they all heard a noise coming from above.

One after the other, the three bears crept up the stairs . . . .

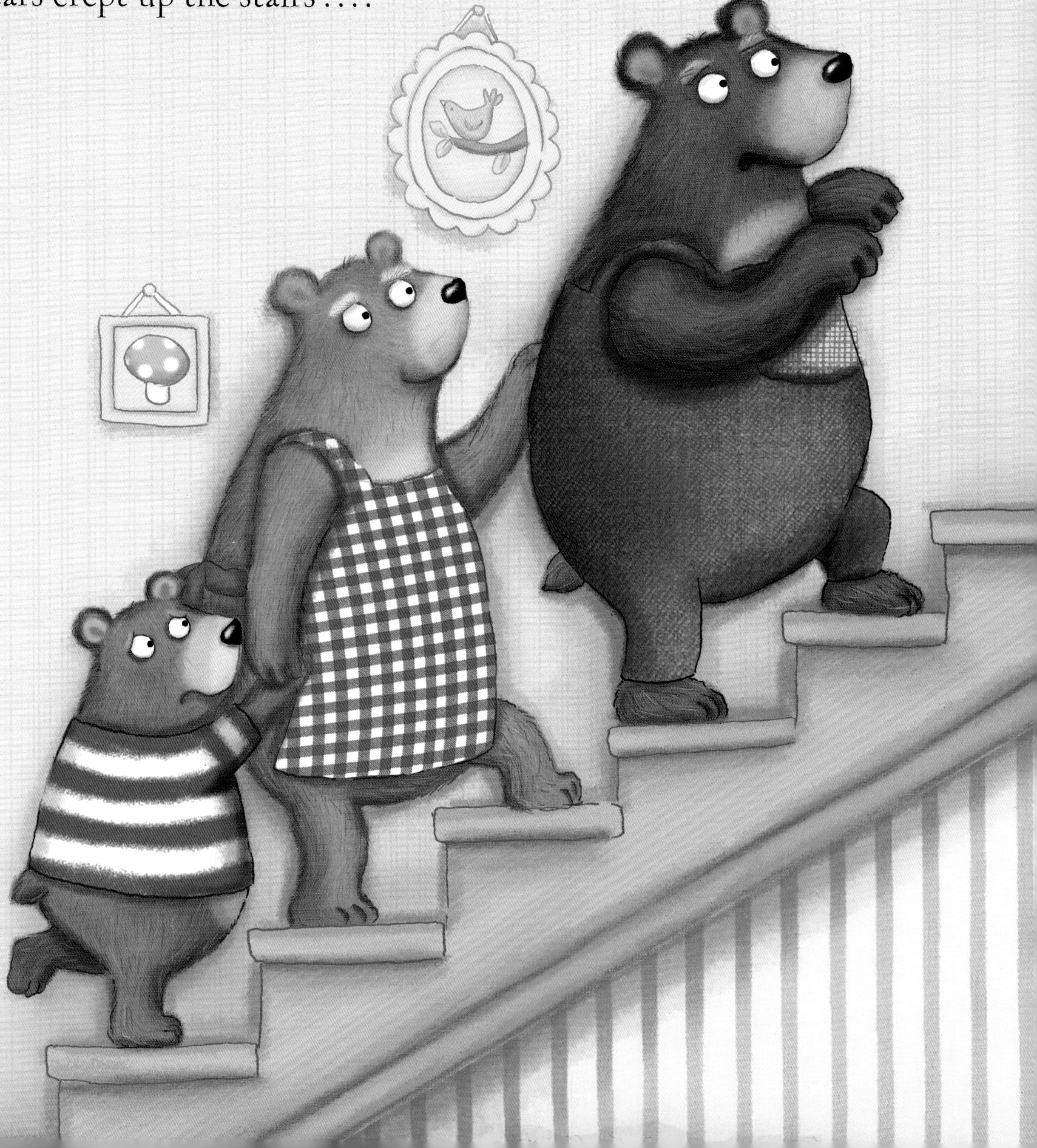

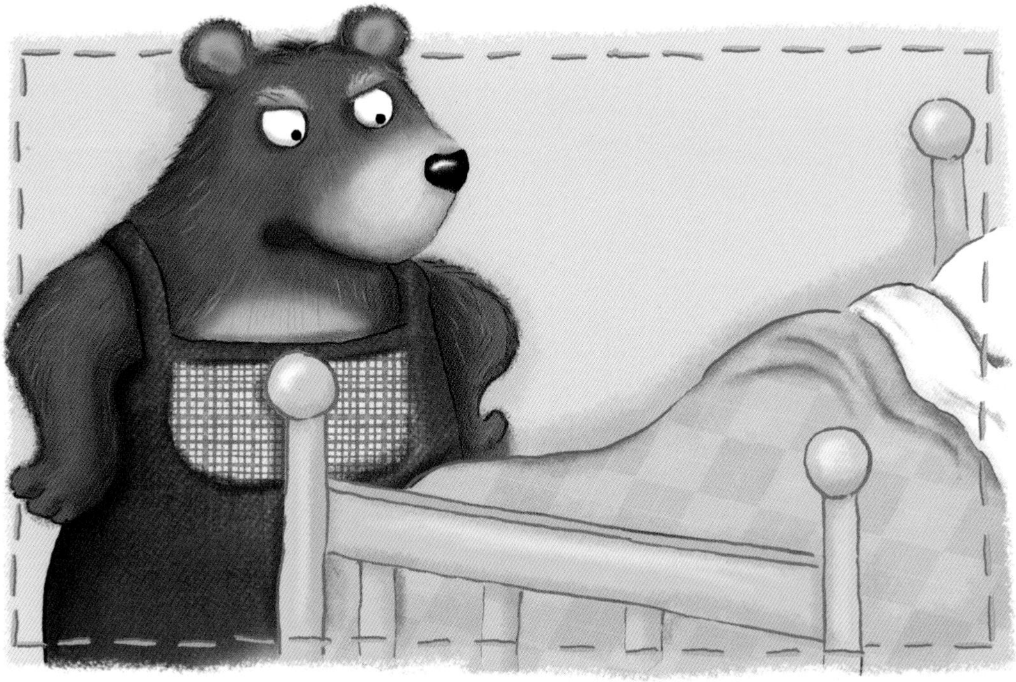

"Someone's been sleeping in my bed," growled Daddy Bear.

"Someone's been sleeping in my bed," gasped Mommy Bear.

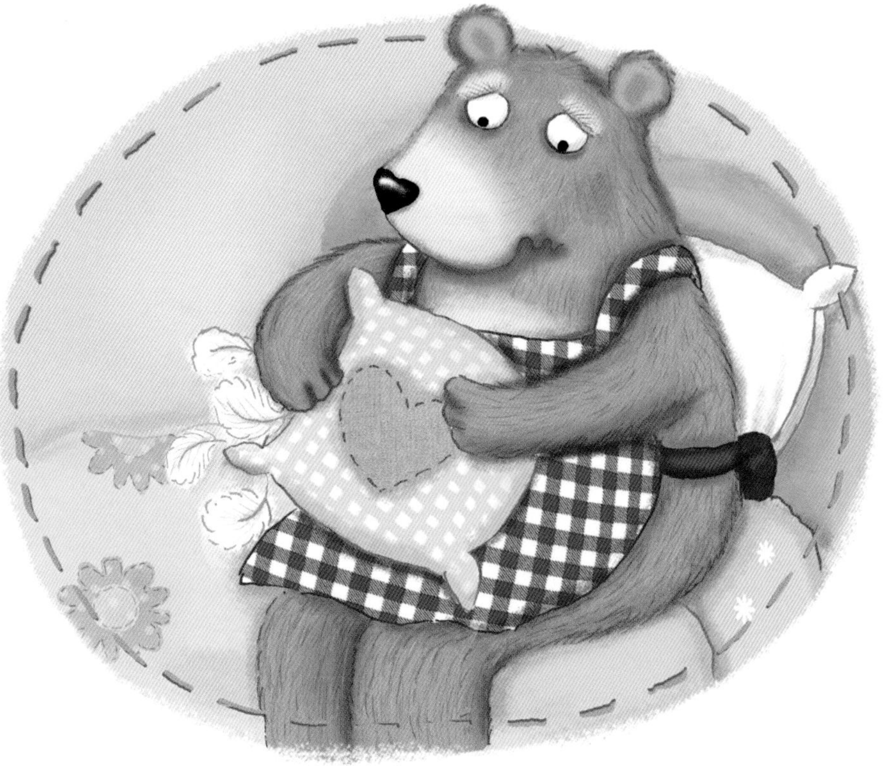

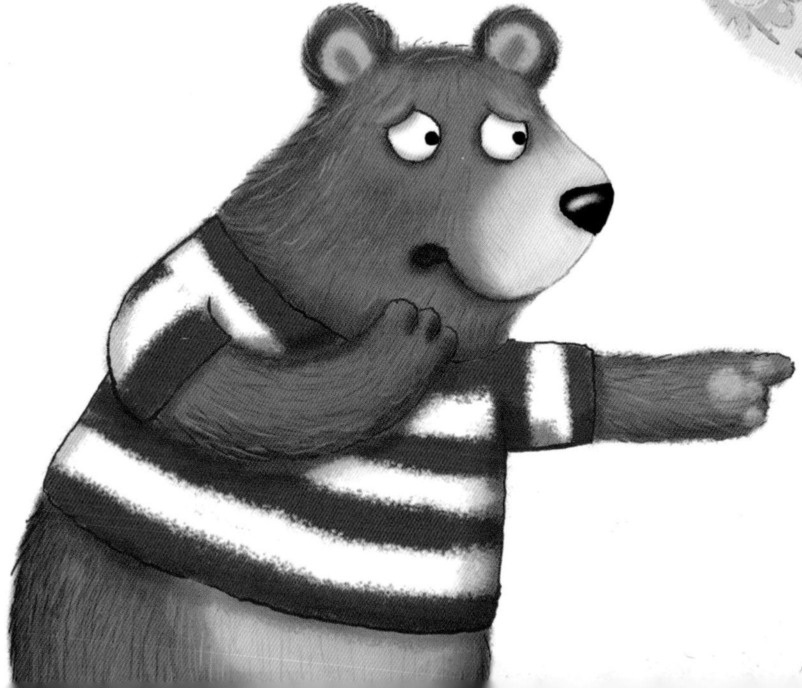

"Someone's been sleeping in **my** bed!" cried Baby Bear . . .

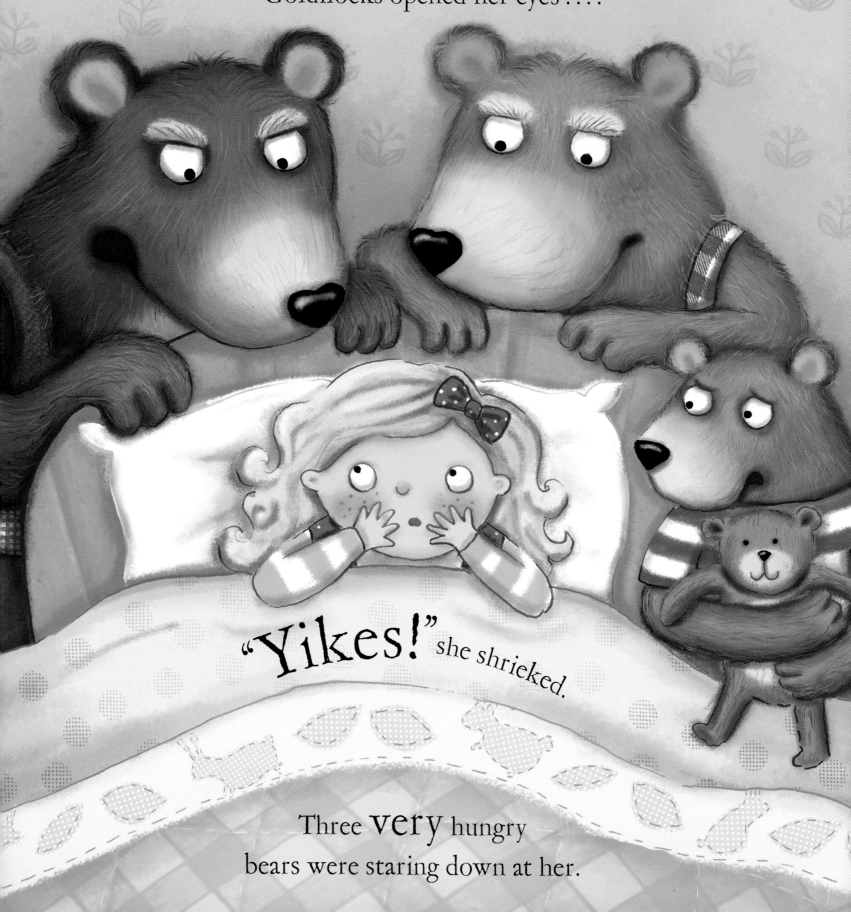

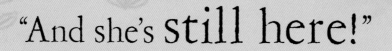

"And she's **still here!**"
Goldilocks opened her eyes....

"Yikes!" she shrieked.

Three **very** hungry
bears were staring down at her.

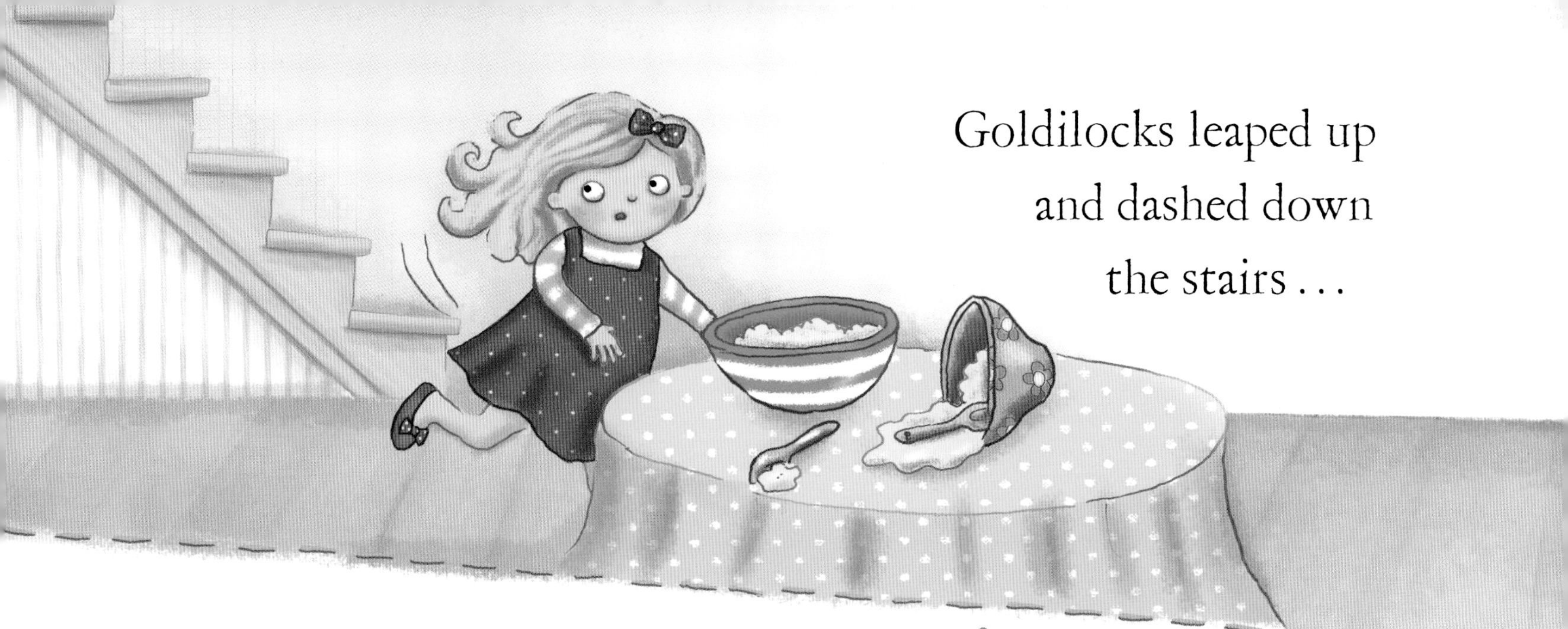

Goldilocks leaped up
and dashed down
the stairs . . .

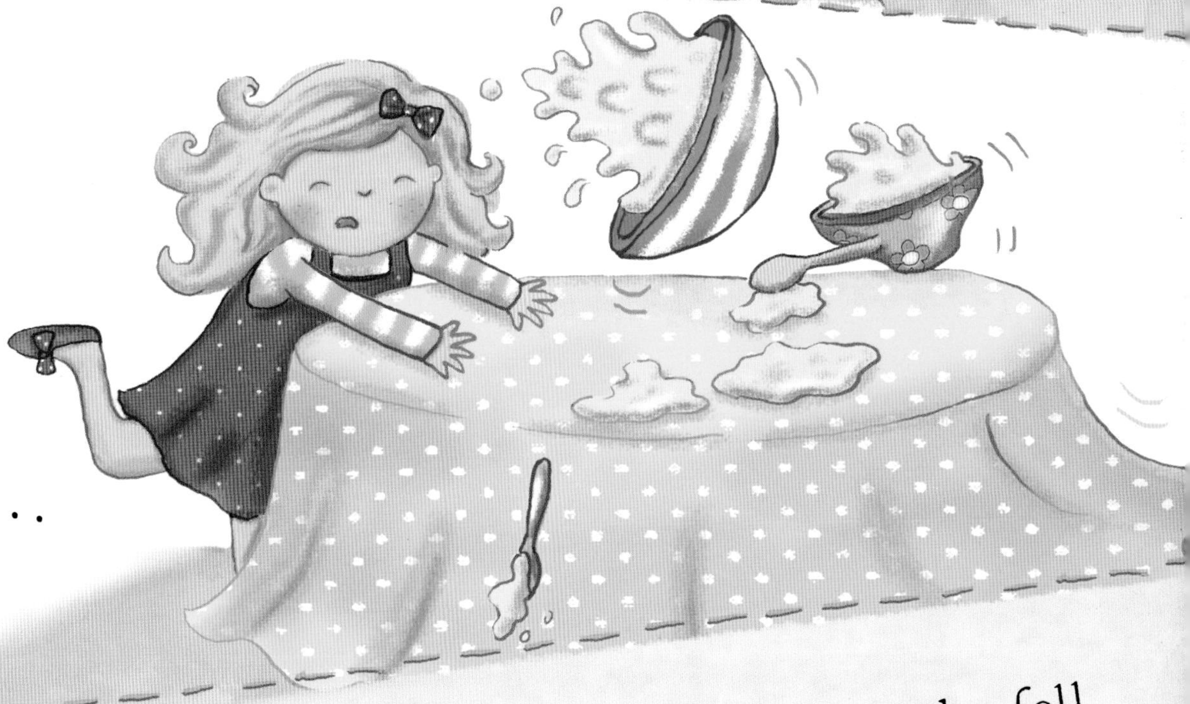

. . . and bumped into
the kitchen table.
SMACK!
The bowls of
porridge flew
up, up, up . . .

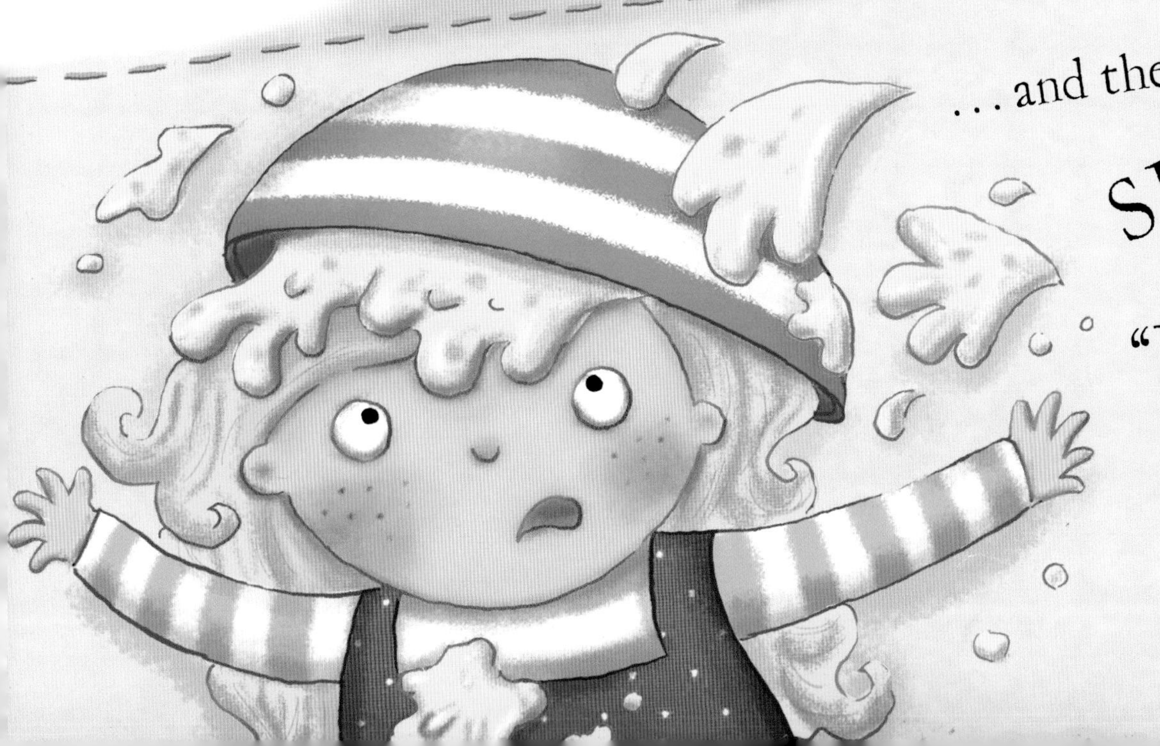

. . . and the gooey porridge fell
SPLAT onto her
golden hair!
"Ewwwww!"
yelped Goldilocks.

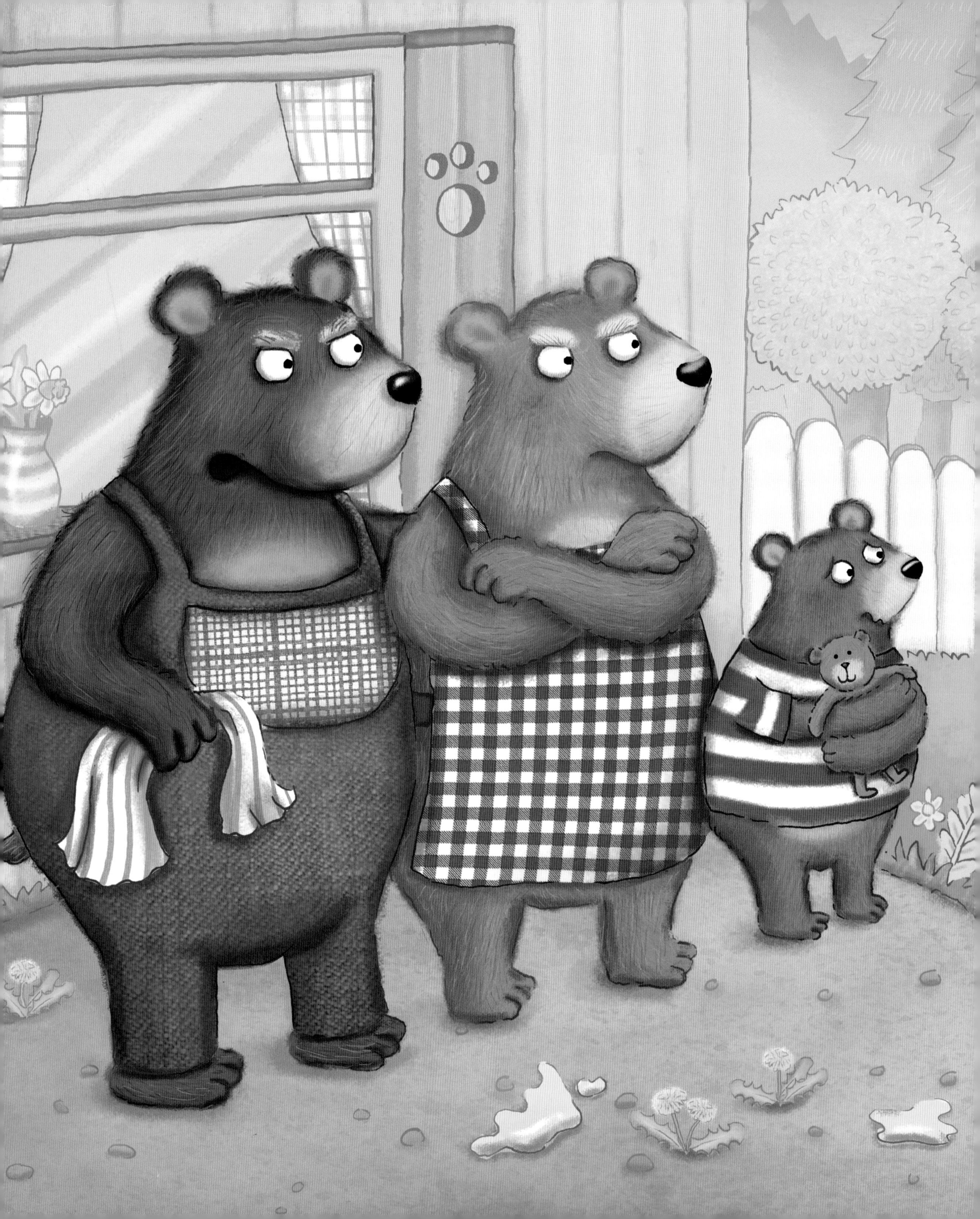

The last the three bears saw of Goldilocks
was her dashing down the path,
leaving a very sticky trail
of porridge behind her.

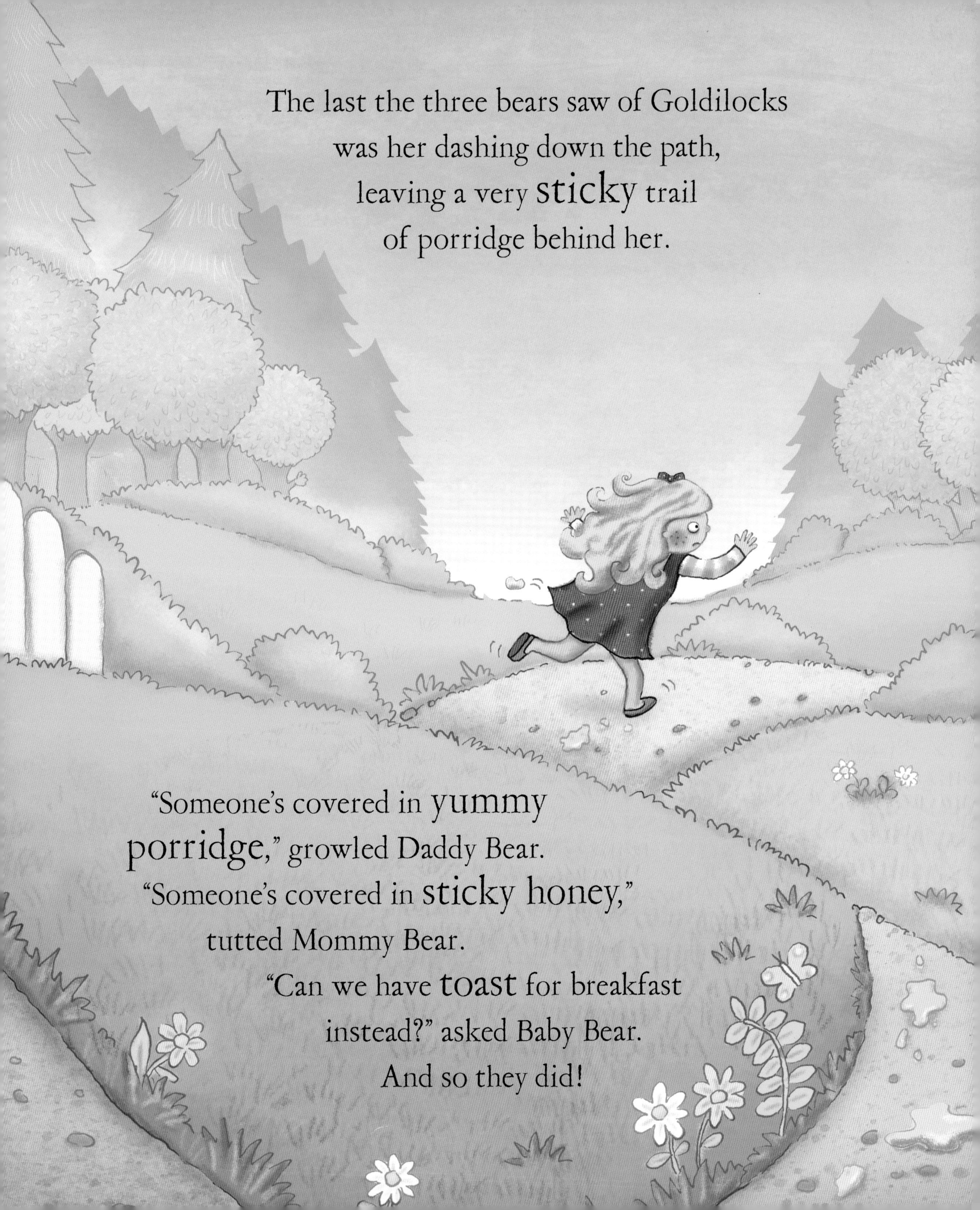

"Someone's covered in yummy
porridge," growled Daddy Bear.
"Someone's covered in sticky honey,"
tutted Mommy Bear.
"Can we have toast for breakfast
instead?" asked Baby Bear.
And so they did!

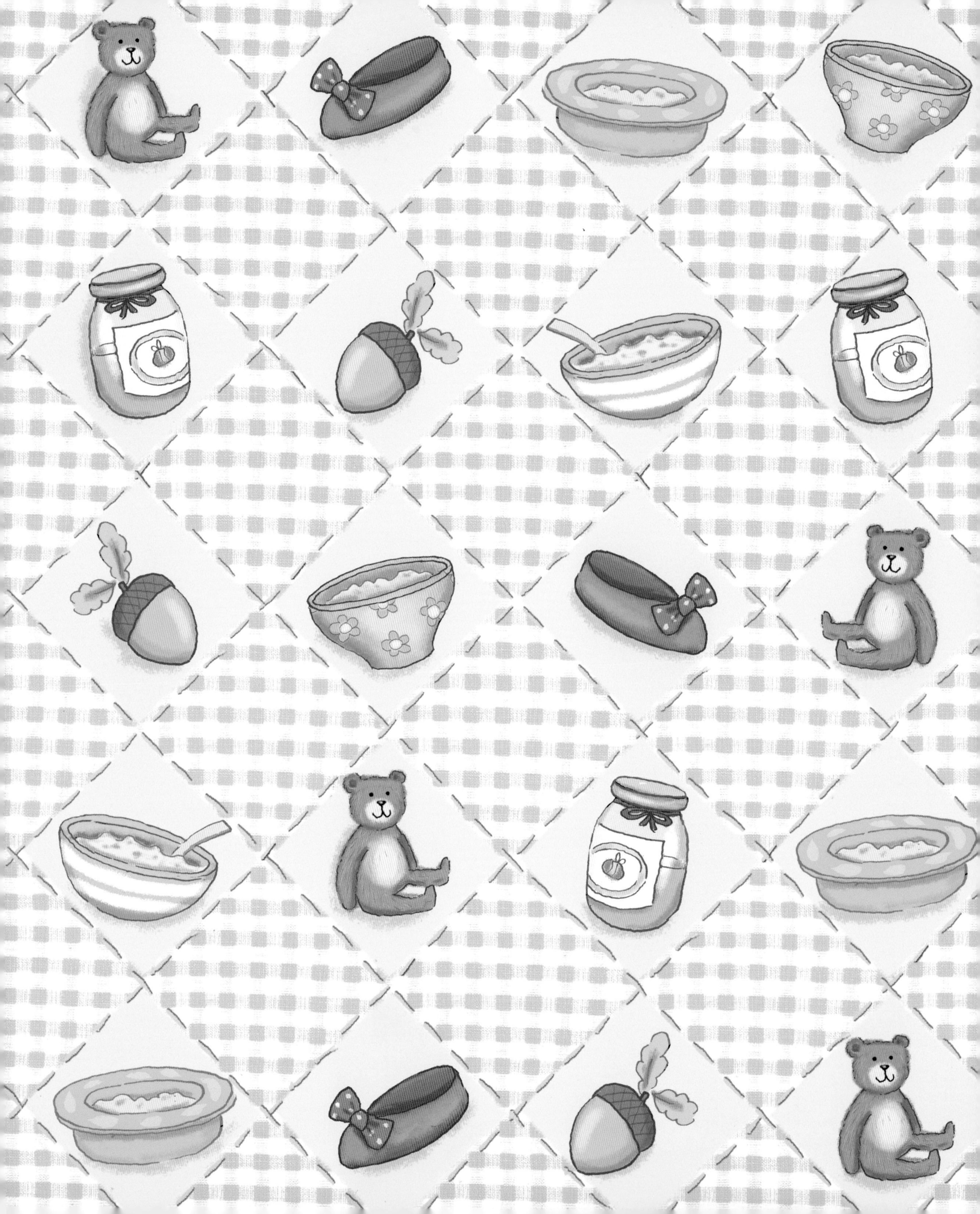

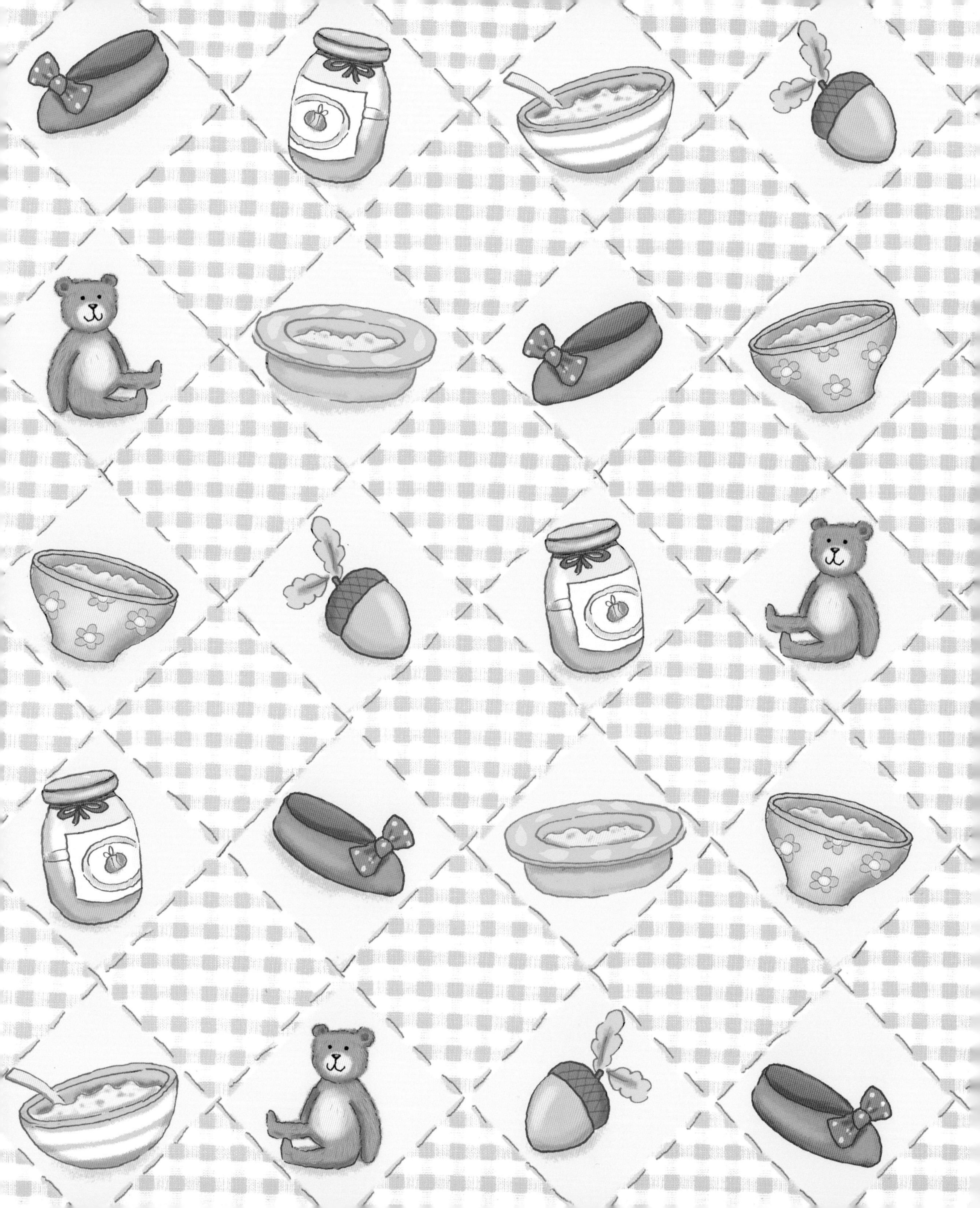

Mara Alperin

Mara has adapted all of the books
in the My First Fairy Tales series, which includes
Little Red Riding Hood, *Goldilocks and the Three Bears*,
Jack and the Beanstalk, and *The Three Billy Goats Gruff*.
As a child, she loved listening to fairy tales and then retelling the stories
to her family and friends. Mara lives in London, England. When not
writing, she enjoys reading, baking, hiking, and
playing Ultimate Frisbee.

Kate Daubney

Kate lives by the sea in North Devon, England, with her partner,
Roger, and her scruffy sidekick, Taz the dog. She graduated with
a degree in illustration and has worked on numerous
children's books, using both digital and traditional media to
create her colorful and quirky illustrations. When she's not busy
illustrating, she loves riding her bike or taking a walk on the beach,
where Taz enjoys chasing the seagulls!